VAPORISE
THE NOVELIZATION

VAPORISE
THE NOVELIZATION

Written by
SEKOU HAMER

Based on characters and stories created in
THE THIRD GRADE

KUUMBA
CREATIONS

Hamer, Sekou
Vaporise: the novelization / Sekou Hamer

Summary: A mild-mannered teenager, James Jenkins, acquires amazing abilities from a mysterious aircraft, and comes to grips with them, while also dealing with his friend, Brian, his crush, Jessica, his Mom and Dad, and keeping it all a secret from those he cares about and those who may wish to cause him harm. Meanwhile, a mysterious evildoer named Dr. Dark begins wreaking havoc in James's town, with the ulterior motive of drawing in James to fulfill a nefarious scheme.

Printed or otherwise manufactured and distributed in the United States of America

First Printing, 2018

ISBN-13: 978-1976846137

Published by Kuumba Creations
January 2018

TABLE OF CONTENTS

DEDICATIONS

Alex Burke and Mrs. Walters, at the Gordon School

This book is firstly dedicated to Alex Burke, Mrs. Walters, and the Gordon School. Before I continue, allow me to preface that I am deeply thankful for Mrs. Walters, and all the things she did for me during my year in her class. I'm thankful for her letting my class be in her room for indoor recess, for having stacks of paper and numerous colored pencils in her shelves that allowed me and my friend to create amazing stories, for reading a made-up synopsis of mine to the entire class at the end of a day. I'm thankful for her having a huge bin of toys specially made to be fidgeted with so students could stay focused, and for allowing us to use those toys even when we didn't really need them. I'm thankful for the sort of "show and tell" book thing she would put on once a week, where we would get up in front of the class and talk about a book we read, I'm thankful for those amazing starfish suits she had in her classroom, of which there were only two, so the class was always fighting over them and eventually evolved to using a sign-up system of who got to wear them that week.

Now, that I've said that, I must further explain myself. While I am thankful to Mrs. Walters, my thanks surrounding her go to something greater: Chance. It amazes me how perfectly that whole year was lined up, all the things that just fell perfectly into place so that VAPORISE could exist. First, my dad gets a job at the Gordon School, as a 7th grade science teacher, so I start going there in the 1st grade. Then, I become friends with Alex, a kid in my class. I get to the 3rd grade, he's in my class again, and we decide to work together on stories and graphic novels, during snack or indoor recess or before Morning Meeting starts. There's so much more in between those three events that spawned the circumstances that VAPORISE was born in, but if I named them all, this dedication would go on forever.

The last person I would like to give their due thanks is my good friend, Alex Burke. Thank you, Alex, for becoming my writing partner in the 3rd grade, for helping me create a number of great stories I still have ideas for even today, VAPORISE being the greatest of them. Much of this book's core content is pulled straight from what we wrote and illustrated: James, Brian, Jessica, his Uncle, the strange Aircraft, Dr. Dark, and so many more. We were such a powerhouse of creativity for those 9 months of school, forming characters and relationships and moments that were so instantly perfect, that even 8 years later, I can't find any way to improve them.

I'm sorry that our paths diverged so early into our partnership. I'm sorry you had to switch to some other school after 3rd grade, I'm sorry we didn't hang out that much after that. I'm sorry I had to move to Philly for high school. I'm sorry I never connected with you on this "Novelization" thing.

I hope you're living a good life, Alex, and I want to thank you one last time for being a half of the great team that put the story of James, Brian, Jessica, and everything else together.

Mr. Walach, at Friends Academy

This book is secondly dedicated to Mr. Walach, at Friends Academy. I'm not thanking him for assigning me the Independent Writing Assignment (IWA), because that was a grade-wide assignment. No matter what teacher I would have ended up with in 7th grade, I would've had to do it.

But, I'm thanking Mr. Walach for the way he taught me. I had him in 6th and 7th grade, and to this day, I have never felt better about how I was doing in a class academically. Mr. Walach was a great teacher, explaining everything he taught slowly, carefully. If he felt like the class was struggling with an activity, or with completing an assignment, he would stop and help us get through, or give us an extension. For something like me who always excelled in English, this sort of class allowed me to take even more time to perfect my writing style and skill, and focus on being creative.

Mr. Walach always had great words to say about my writing assignments, which motivated me to keep doing it and work to improve myself, and it turned writing to one of my favorite pastimes. Not just writing, but creating in general. Mr. Walach giving my essay an A was great for my grade. But, when Mr. Walach gave one of my creative writing assignments, like a poetry collection or a short story, an A, those were the most pivotal moments of my life as a creator.

When the IWA was due, I handed Mr. Walach roughly the first half of this book. It was much less worked on and refined than it is now, but for a 7th grader, it was no small feat. Back then, it was 40-something pages long, font size 12. I was so blown away by what I had done. I handed it in, knowing how good it was and knowing that I was probably going to get an A because of previous assignments I had handed in. When he handed it back to me about a month later, I got an A for creative content, and an A+ for writing skill. This is the proudest moment of my life, being graded so well on a purely creative work, a passion project. From then on, I was sure I was a good writer.

I talked to Mr. Walach at the end of the year. I had come back to get the copy of the assignment that he had graded. I wanted it so I could make the edits and improve them. Mr. Walach said something along the lines of, "Sekou, I think you should really try and finish this. And when you do, send me a copy. I'd love to read it." From then on, I was sure I would finish this book.

So, Mr. Walach, I hope this book lands in your hands. I hope you read it, and see all the ways I've improved this story, and the ways I've improved as a writer. Above all, I hope you enjoy it. You're one of the big reasons why it exists. Thank you.

Many Teachers, at Germantown Friends School

This book is lastly dedicated to several faculty members at Germantown Friends School. Allow me to list them all and their relevance to the completion of this novel.

Coming to GFS, finishing this book looked very distant, like something that I wouldn't be done with until I graduated. Then, in January, during my freshman year, **Sara Primo** held a Creative Writing Class. This class is where I wrote 80% of the second half of this book.

The next year, **Robin Friedman** held her Creating Writing Class. This one was much more like a "class" and less a free period for people to just work on whatever they were working on. In this class, I got to read parts of chapters I was working on editing, and I got so many great comments, some constructive, most just positive. The most important comments to be were from Robin herself. All she told me is that she thought it was good, and she couldn't wait to see what I might do with it, but, praise is far more resonant coming from a faculty member than just my friends, peers, and fellow classmates.

Adam Hotek receives a dedication somewhat inadvertently and somewhat undeservingly. I once emailed Adam about being one of the speakers at Writer's Assembly my Sophomore year, where people stand up in front of the school something they've written. In the email, I sent him the first half of Chapter I. He reviewed it, and told me he thought it was great, and he would try and get me into the Assembly. Then, one day I found out the assembly was THAT day, leaving me confused as to how I wasn't notified whether I was accepted or not. I ran into another teacher, Alex Levin, who told me he would look for Adam after I told him what happened. The assembly rolled around, and I got no word from Adam. Later after the assembly, Adam found me. He apologized, saying he just forgot about the email, never passing it on to appropriate people. Adam told me that the excerpt I sent him really was good, and he would make sure that I spoke at the next Writer's Assembly. Adam is important to me finishing the book because he helped spread the word of it. Thanks to him, more teachers knew I was working on it, and wanted to see it completed. Also, knowing that I would be speaking at the next Writer's Assembly has motivated me to make the book as good as I possibly can.

Lastly, I want to thank **June Gondi and Alex Levin**, because of how much of advocates they were of me finishing this book. Ever since June found out about this book from Adam Hotek, she's been telling me to finish it every time she sees me, and been sending me emails about writing contests and other such things that I might be interested in. Alex has been so nice to me and supportive of me since I came to the school, and this book, as well and anything else I've written, is no exception. I want to thank them for keeping the book on my mind. I don't think I would've NOT completed it, but it definitely would've taken me longer if not for their constant support. Also, I want to thank them for how supportive they were of my writing, having only heard of and read an excerpt from one of my works.

To those mentioned, thank you all. This is from and for you.

THE NOVELIZATION

Ch. I: THE EVENT

James Jenkins was once a mild-mannered teenager. But, his perfectly normal life was changed forever during one summer. Although this summer, in most respects, was just like any other summer for James. After about seven weeks of sitting around, hanging out with friends, playing video games, trying to text girls and them not responding, James had arrived at his favorite part of every summer. He was out in the wilderness, on his annual two-week camping trip with his Uncle Vlad, this being the ninth anniversary of it. It was the last day of their retreat. They sat by a fire in the middle of a large field. A small mountain range overlooked their setup. Large grass hills were around them and within walking distance.

The last two weeks had been full of two things: dangerous activities and seeing unbelievable exhibitions of nature. James and his uncle had satiated their want for adventure, and so they wanted to end their retreat with something that was relaxing, and that surely wouldn't wind up being dangerous or unbelievable. They decided to set up camp in the middle of the biggest field they could find, lie on their backs, and look up at the night sky. As they looked on, laser-focused, they became wary of the stillness of everything around them, and wanted to believe that they could see each star moving in its own minute direction.

"Stars are amazing," Vlad said. Uncle Vlad was short for Uncle Vladimir. His hair was dark brown and curly, grown out into an unpicked afro. You couldn't tell anyway, because he was wearing a large orange hat he brought from home. He didn't normally have facial hair, but every year on these trips to the woods with his nephew he would never shave, and so he would acquire some stubble, of an unevenness which explained why he was otherwise clean shaven. He had a plaid mulberry sweater on under his windbreaker of the same color. He wore light brown khakis and a black belt to hold them up, the cuffs of which still slumping down to the sides of his beige shoes.

"Yeah, I guess," James said. "I mean, they're pretty bright." James was of an above-average height, to where he looked down at most of his family members but up at anybody else. His skin was a smooth, milky brown and without a noticeable blemish. His hair was jet black, curly and cut short. Today, he was wearing a regular pair of jeans, and a red t-shirt under his loose-fitting, black, zip-up sweatshirt. He had turned 15 about month prior.

They weren't saying much, just looking up. Until, James broke the blissful silence.

"Vlad?" James called out.

"Yeah?" his uncle replied.

14

"Am... Am I gonna... I mean... Is high school gonna be tough for me? Like, how was high school for you?"

"For me?" Vlad repeated to himself. "I mean, I didn't think much of it at the time. You know, I remember there being talk of who was popular, and whoever that was usually the best athletes on whatever team was in season, so it wasn't the same for long. But, I didn't associate with those people. Ever, really. So, popularity wasn't a thing in my neck of the woods." Vlad paused as his nephew took this in. He could tell that James was feeling somewhat reassured already. He continued, "I would say that the worst thing I ever had to deal with was when I was a senior. Because, your dad was a freshman and he was quickly known as the best player on our school's basketball team. Now, I was never on the team in my high school career, but I still somehow got made fun of because people thought my little brother was better than me at basketball." James laughed. Vlad continued, "I mean, not people, just my friends. It wasn't like the entire school was dumping their lunch on me. But, anyway, you'll never have to deal with that, because you don't have any siblings." At this, James's eyes craned away from this uncle beside him and back to the stars. "What's funny is our school's team wasn't really all that great. So, your dad being the best player really didn't mean anything. Cause, when he came home and we played, he never even touched the ball once I got it. But that just goes to show you what the kids at my school considered good.... anything, really." James and Vlad had a good laugh. After some silence, Vlad began again with,

"My overarching point in all this is-"

"Vlad, I get it," James said.

"You do, do you?" Vlad said.

"Sorta."

"You've just gotta remember that high school isn't the end-all-be-all of your existence. Just because high school sucks for you doesn't mean life is gonna suck, and the opposite is just as true. It all seems like a big deal now, because, you know, everybody's gonna be older than you and know more than you. But, it's really not. I swear, by the time you… maybe even as soon as you're a sophomore, you'll look back and say, 'why was I fussing over this?'"

"You sure?" James asked.

"Really," Vlad replied. "I swear, you're not going to have anything to worry about in high school."

James smiled, and both settled back into their positions on the ground, facing the night sky. Then, James was moved to speak once more.

"Vlad?" James said.

"Yeah?" his uncle replied.

"What's the most you think I'll have to worry about?" James asked. "Like, what sort of things?"

Vlad thought for a bit, and then said, "It's really what you make it, James. It depends on what you decide to do. Like, if you go out for a lot of different activities, and want to excel in all your classes, you'll be under a lot of pressure. But…If you do nothing extracurricular or outside of school or any sports, and you don't care about your grades, then, you'll be relatively stress-free."

"Okay," James said. "So -"

"So, listen to me. No matter what you do in high school, I can guarantee that you will be able to get through it. I'm serious. I guarantee that."

"Really?" James asked.

Vlad leaned a shoulder towards James, facing him while lying on his side. He patted James's shoulder, saying, "I'm sure of it."

Then, suddenly, something catastrophic happened. The utter silence of the camp was broken by a quiet, slowly increasing whistle. An aircraft, barely distinguishable from their distance, glided across the sky, cascading over the two's line of sight. As it lowered, James and Vlad slowly rolled their necks forward to see where it was going. Then it stopped flying forward, and began to hover over one of the distant glass hills, Then, it fell straight down. It landed silently on the hill, quiet enough that James and Vlad wondered if it even crashed or it was just a shaky landing. It had created a deep crater in the hill, but the two didn't know that yet.

"Whoa," James said. "What was that?"

Vlad looked at James, then turned back to the hill to say, "I don't know."

"Should we go see what that was?" James asked, curiosity consuming his common sense. "You know, get a closer look?"

Vlad, looking at the wreckage, slowly said, "....... Yeah?" He must have been just as curious as James. "Also, whoever was flying that thing probably needs some help."

James and Vlad slowly picked themselves up off the blanket. And then, a great, giant explosion took place on the hill, so large that it reflected into the sky as an orange glow that blinded the two from view of the stars behind it. James and Vlad fell back onto the blanket, cowering and covering their ears. The explosion was fiery and bright, and among the fire rising there was a glowing, green liquid.

James and Vlad didn't move for a minute. Then, James said, "Well, they're probably not alive anymore." He said this jokingly, but Vlad didn't laugh and refrain from his serious demeanor, and soon James realized that he should be far more scared than he was.

The liquid began dripping down to hill. From this distance, the hill now looked like a green, molten lava cake. James and Vlad were astonished, their gaze not leaving the smoking wreckage. It was still bubbling. Neither of them truly realizing the weight of their situation and what encountering that aircraft could potentially mean for them, they stood up and, together, walked towards it.

As James and his uncle got closer to the crater, they slowed to an inching pace. By the time they had reached the foot of the hill, the green light coming from it was blinding. James still wanted to see more. He moved up the hill, beads of sweat dripping from his chin with every step. Vlad followed. Now he was at the edge of the crater made by the rock. It was a perfect circle. Most of the dirt was still brown, but some of it had a pulsing red glare. Now able to see into the crater, James saw that whatever crashed did not contain any human, as inside of it was nothing but circuit boards and wires. James leaned so slightly forward, and Vlad, fed up, darted an arm and grabbed him by the back of the neck.

"Alright, James," Vlad said sternly. "Let's move away from the hill and call somebody who can deal with this."

"One sec," James turned to Vlad to say.

Vlad sighed in distress. "James, c'mon, we NEED to go."

As James turned back, his foot slid into the soft red dirt. Once his foot lost support, his whole body came falling. Vlad's eyes widened as he reached out to James, fingers spread and curled like an animal's claws. As James rolled down into the crater, the green light reflected more and more on his face. "No!" Uncle Vlad screamed, falling to his knees and desperately trying to grab at him. "James, get out of there! JAMES!"

It was too late for James to get up. The dirt was entangling him like a mummy. He was rolling too fast to be stopped. His body hit the aircraft, and came to a halt, as the green liquid surfaced over his body. His uncle screamed again, "NO!" Then, the liquid overflowed over the whole hill, sending Vlad running back down to the ground. He ran back to their setup to use his phone to call for help, green residue still dripping off his pant cuffs and sizzling.

V

James awoke in a hospital. He was on a bed, with an IV in each of his arms. He tried to look up or around, but his neck hurt too much. In fact, his whole body hurt. He felt like he was about to die, the pain was so intense. He heard a subtle ambience in the room, the muffled whispers of some nearby people.

"Don't worry, you're not dead," Said a fuzzy voice. Again, James tried to crane his neck to the side, but he couldn't. "Well, obviously you're not dead, or else you wouldn't hear me. And at that point, why would I even say anything to you? I mean, you're dead, right?"

The voice's source walked around to face James. The voice belonged to a man. He slightly lowered himself and leaned over to be in James's line of sight. As his vision and hearing focused back, he saw it was a doctor. He was tall, had very short black hair and was wearing thick glasses. He had a white coat on, one that looked like it belonged on a scientist and not a doctor. This doctor was black, which intrigued James, because he had never had a black doctor.

"Please, don't stress yourself," said the voice. "I am – uh – I meant to say that my name is, uh –" he hesitated, looking at him weirdly. "Let's - uh - try that again. Hello, James. My name is... uh... Dr. Dean."

"Nice to meet you," James said.

"I guess we all mess up on our last names sometimes, right?" The self-proclaimed Dr. Dean laughed at his joke. Really laughed. James's muscles were starting to loosen up. As James began lifting his chest, the doctor placed a hand on him to keep him on the bed. "Now, before I can let you rest again, I need to ask you a few questions." James obliged. "Okay, first question: ……. Do you remember at all what happened to you?" Dr. Dean pointed at a man with a clipboard and mouthed some words. James

20

looked over and saw Uncle Vlad, sitting down in a chair. Then, he saw both his parents next to Vlad. James felt both reassurance and the exact opposite.

James remembered what happened quite vividly, despite his state of mind. He described the event. "So, I was camping with my uncle and then this....... this metal thing....... I think it was a ship....... crashed into a nearby hill. We went to go explore the crash site. I kept walking forward.......forward....... and then, I accidentally....... Uh....... my foot....... uh... - That's all I remember. I think I hit my head on something. And now-"

"And now you're here. Yes, yes. Next question," Dr. Dean said. He seemed in a hurry. He turned to look at the man with the clipboard again. James couldn't see the doctor's face, but based on the frightened face of the man with the clipboard, Dr. Dean wasn't looking too nice. "Do you feel any... built-up heat in your core? Any pressure?"

"No," said James. "I feel perfectly normal. Minus the muscle pain. I feel like I need to stretch."

Dr. Dean seemed a bit distraught with the information that he had received. "Okay," said the doctor. "If that's all you have to say, then I guess that's all I needed," he said. "To hear," he quickly added. "Well, anyway, I've already explained exactly what's going on with you to your folks over there. But, you don't know yet, do you?"

"Obviously not, I've been asleep," James said.

"Well, when you rolled into the crater, and you came in contact with the crashed flying object, the green, glowing liquid inside of it passed an unnatural energy into

21

your body. We extracted as much as we could; at least, enough that your skin wasn't green anymore-"

"My skin was green?" James interjected.

"But whatever that liquid was, it put you in a state of paralysis and limited brain activity. You've been in a coma for the last 3 days while we've been extracting the energy from your body."

"What kind of technology would you even use to do that?" James asked. "I mean, I'm not complaining or anything, but that sounds kinda farfetched. Also, MY SKIN WAS GREEN?"

"You wouldn't understand from a single 5-minute explanation."

"I actually think I *would* understand just fine if you'd tell me."

"Anyway, you should know that you can't leave yet. Because some of this weird, foreign energy is still in you."

"Still in me?" James exclaimed. "Can I get some specifics? Like, how much? Am I gonna need surgery or have I already had surgery and it didn't solve anything?"

"Well, no. It's not that bad at all. It's sort of like a common sickness, like a virus. Your immune system should take care of it overtime. If it doesn't, which I doubt would happen, we'll be seeing you periodically to do tests and try a multitude of solving methods, so that it can officially be eliminated well before it becomes a problem that can't be fixed with antibacterial agents. It is nothing - and I mean nothing - to worry about."

"Okay." James looked out the window. He saw that it was daytime. Then, he looked around the room. Just then, his parents and Uncle Vlad came in. They rushed to the sides of his bed and leaned in to give him a big hug. "OW, guys, I'm still sore."

"Honey, I'm so glad you're awake," his mother said. "We've been so worried about you."

"Okay, Mom," James said.

James's father was quiet until James's mother gave him a look. "Uh... Good to have you back," he said begrudgingly. Vlad remained mute.

"Please!" Dr. Dean nearly shouted, "Can I calmly explain to my patient what his situation is." James's family was startled. They scurried out in a line through the door and closed it behind them, residing behind the large glass window with its blinds slightly opened on the inside of the room.

"Uh, why was there green liquid in that aircraft, anyway?" James asked, as if this doctor would know anything about it.

"Beats me," Dr. Dean said, darting his eyes, "I just know about you. Honestly, I'm just glad you're still alive." He laughed at himself. A little too much, to the point that James wasn't sure what he was joking about. "So, I would say: rest for another day of so, and we'll see if you can walk around the halls a bit. Okay." He patted James on the back.

"So, when am I going to get out?"

"We've just got to get a couple more blood tests and complete some muscle exercises to fully insure that you can recover and *don't* still feel any heat in your chest or muscles. We'll make sure your systems are running at full speed again." The doctor's hand moved up from James's back to rest on James's shoulder.

"WHEN?" James asked again, louder.

"In a week or so." Dr. Dean said, a hand still resting on James's shoulder, "I will do everything I can to keep you safe."

Dr. Dean winked and left the room in a frenzy, the man with the clipboard following close after.

James's family came back in and returned to his bedside.

Vlad spoke, "James, I am so sorry. I should have stopped you. It was so dangerous, I don't know what I was thinking letting you go up that hill. I'm sorry."

"Vlad, it's okay," James said. "I'm not dead, right? And I'm also not still sick or anything. So, I'm fine. It's fine, Vlad."

"Alright," Vlad said. He stepped back and looked at James's parents with a remorseful look.

"Do you think you'll be okay by September?"

"Yeah, of course," James said, slowly leaning back down onto his bed. "I hope." He really didn't want to miss the first day of school.

Ch. II: **V**ACATION'S END

It had been exactly 7 days since James woke up in the hospital. Since, then, he'd gotten a lot better. His muscles weren't hurting, and his skin hadn't looked green since the previous week. Things were looking good for James.

James woke up on his first day of school, September 1st, and got dressed in his favorite shirt and best-fitting pants. As he came down the stairs, his parents both greeted him. He went to the kitchen. After grabbing two slices of bread from the cupboard and placing each in the slot of his toaster, he left the kitchen and sat down at the dining table, where his parents were.

"Feeling alright, James," his father said.

James nodded subtly. He was nervous, but only because it was technically a new school for him. The only person he knew coming to this school from his old one was his best friend, Brian. Besides him, he was gonna be all alone. He'd have to make new friends and all, but what really worried him was the girls. James had never talked to a girl about anything other than homework or a TV show. If James was going to be at least normal in high school, he'd have to talk to girls more. James wasn't really ready for that.

As he looked aimlessly around the room, his eye was caught on someone walking right outside his window. It was actually Brian, about to knock on his kitchen window to have him come outside so they could walk to school. James popped the toaster and grabbed his dry, half-toasted bread, and a banana, as he flew out of the kitchen to the living room and opened the front door.

As one of his feet passed through the door frame, his mom yelled from the kitchen, "Honey, be careful."

"Okay, mom!" James shouted back. He closed the door behind him and walked out past his lawn to the sidewalk. James walked up to meet Brian's path on the sidewalk, and continued walking next to him.

James noticed that Brian had grown two inches since he last saw him. Other than that, he was the same: piercing blue eyes, long and slender neck, blond hair. Brian and James had been best friends since 1st grade, and they'd been in the same classes for most of their years since then. Because James and Brian lived close enough to their high school, they made plans earlier in the summer to walk there every day. Today would be the first of many morning walks and talks.

"So, how was your summer?" Brian laughed as he spoke.

"What do you mean 'how was my summer'?" said James. "You were with me for most of it. We hung out every other day for like, 4 weeks straight."

"No. I meant, like, how was the hospital?"

"Oh, okay. Cause, you didn't say that. You said, 'How was your summer?'".

"Well, I just didn't know how to introduce a question like that."

"You could just ask it. I mean, I'm wasn't traumatized about it."

"Well, from your texts, it sounded like something out of a comic book."

"Whatever. Believe it or not, it happened. Anyway, I mean, for my first time in the hospital, it was a good experience. The nurses were nice -"

"Were the nurses, like -?"

"What?"

"You know?"

"No, I don't. You're not saying words."

"Were they hot?"

James sighed. "No, Brian. I wasn't really focused on that. I was more focused on being in the hospital, for my intense muscle pains."

"Okay, jeez I was just curious."

"Also, most of my nurses were guys, anyway-"

"Okay, so, anyway, let me get this straight: you were camping with Vlad, and a meteor crashed on a hill right next to you-"

"No, not a meteor," James interjected. "It was like a remote-control plane thing."

27

"Okay," Brain continued. "So, the plane crashed….. and then exploded. And there was green, glowing liquid. And then you walked over to it, and you slipped into the liquid, and then you woke up in the hospital."

"Yeah," James said.

"Okay, so……. Which writing contest are you sending this too?"

"Brian, I wasn't joking. You know that."

"Actually, you probably hit your head on the rock in the woods or something BEFORE you guys were at the campfire. And then everything that happened after that was a dream.

"Everything after that?" James questioned. "So, the whole story?"

"Yeah, pretty much."

"Whatever," James said. "I know you believe me."

"And also, you say they had *tried* to get as much out as possible, which then begs the quest -"

"No, but then, later, they did get it all out. If they didn't, I'd still be in the hospital."

"No, but still," Brian said. "What if they didn't get it all *again*?" Brian's eyes bulged as he stared at James, imitating a zombie or just some scary guy. "What if it gives you special powers. You could be a superhero."

"You're pissing me off now," James said.

"Seriously, you could turn into a giant green monster, or have super speed, or fly."

James rolled his eyes, "Did you just binge-watch every marvel movie?"

28

"Where's your imagination, bro?" asked Brian. "Haven't you ever wanted to be a superhero?"

"Yeah, but… Brian, we're in high school. We've got to let go of our childish fant-"

"Whoa," Brian said, interrupting James. "Who's that?"

"Who?" James looked in Brian's direction. "Whoa."

"Yeah, I know right?"

As they crept onto the outskirts of their school's campus, they saw a beautiful girl. She had long, black hair, flowing freely from her head and dancing in curls around her neck and shoulders. She had caramel-colored skin, she had round, glossy hazel-colored eyes, she had a thin nose that sunlight glistened from, she had full, smooth lips on her small mouth, open in a smile that showed her bright white teeth. She was perfect. For James, anyway.

"Uh, were you at New Student Orientation yesterday?" James asked Brian.

"Yeah," Brian replied. "I saw you, but you were just sitting with your family."

"Was she there? Cause, I didn't see her."

"Probably not," said Brian. "I think I would've noticed a girl like that."

"Wow," James said.

"I know right? She's gorgeous." Brian saw that James's gaze hadn't left the girl since they first saw her. "Hey, why don't you go talk to her?"

"C'mon, Brian. It's day one. I don't wanna screw up the next four years in the first few minutes."

"How would you screw up the next four years?"

"I don't know. I just would. You know I'm not good with girls. I'd probably trip over something while walking over to her, and everyone would see it, and I'd be known as *that* guy. Or, maybe I would ask her out, and she'd say no, and then she'd tell all her friends and then every girl in the school would know and - Whatever, man. I don't *have* to do anything."

"I'm not saying you have to ask her out. And I'm not saying you have to make a *good* impression. I'm just saying you should talk to her. You'll never be good at something if you never do it."

The girl walked into the school building, out of sight from both James and Brian.

James sighed. "Yeah, okay," he said. "If I bump into her, I'll start a conversation."

"There you go, James," Brian said, as they walked towards the school, "It's time you start putting yourself out there."

James and Brian began walking to the school. Though James gave off the air that he was above it, he was fantasizing about meeting her. James had a mission to talk to that girl, and he wasn't gonna take no for an answer.

V

"No," said a student to James, "I don't know where the campus maps are. My friend gave me this one and I don't know where he got his." The student walked away, leaving James feeling discouraged.

"I guess we'll just have to find our own way around," Brian said. James and Brian continued down the main hall. They had gotten their locker combinations, and were mainly focused on seeing if they were near each other. The hallways were crowded and full of commotion, yet still felt oddly spaced out and reserved.

"OH! Here's mine," Brian said, "164." He diverged his path from James as he curled towards his reserved locker. He started trying his combination, when he turned back to James to say, "Good luck finding yours."

"Okay," James said, as he began to walk away.

"Oh, and good luck with that girl," Brian added.

"Yeah, yeah, whatever."

James figured that if Brian's locker number started with a 1 and was one the first floor, and his locker number started with a 2, then he must be one floor above. He found a stairwell, and made his way up. He reached the second floor, and started his search again. He, sure enough, found his locker, 276, and tried his combo. It worked. As it was only the first day, he had nothing more than a notebook and a couple pencils in his locker, so he closed it and turned to leave. Just then, he bumped into a person, causing them to drop their calculator.

"Sorry," said James, "I'm a klutz." The person laughed. It was a girl's laugh. James bent down to pick up the calculator. As he came back up, he looked at the girl, and saw that it was the same girl he had seen outside.

"It's okay," she said, smiling.

James was ecstatic, but restrained himself from breaking into the wide, gaping smile he wanted to. "Yeah - uhhh - sorry about that," he said.

"It's fine. It wasn't a big deal at all," she said, laughing. "Also, can I get my calculator back, please?"

"Oh, yeah, right," he said, noticing he had had it in a tight grip since he picked it up. Handing it over, he said, "No problem."

"Okay," the girl said, looking at her hand as the calculator was placed in it.

"So, what class do you have first?" James asked, after a period of awkward silence. "Algebra, perhaps?" he said, pointing at the calculator. He was trying to make small talk and beginning to fail.

"Yeah. Why, do you have it too?"

"Yeah."

"What a coincidence," she said, trying to put the calculator in a side pouch of her bag without looking behind her.

"Maybe we should walk there?" James proposed.

"Well, we can't fly, so-"

"No, I mean like, *we* should walk to class. You know, together."

"I mean, that doesn't really matter though," she said. "I mean, since we're both headed there anyway."

"My point exactly?" James questioned himself as the words left his mouth. "Whatever, I was just asking. You know, if you don't have anywhere else you need to be, cause that's just where I'm headed now."

"Yeah, whatever," the girl said with the vocal

equivalent of a shoulder shrug, as they both started walking.

"Hey, do you have a campus map?" James asked. "Cause I couldn't manage to get one, and I have no idea which building is the math building."

"Yeah, I got one," she said, handing it to him, "I got it near the front doors at some table."

"Ohhh, I came in a different way."

"Why?" the girl asked.

"I was just -" James couldn't admit he was trying to avoid confronting her. "I don't know, I guess. Oh, my name's James, by the way." He held out a hand.

"Nice to meet you, James," she said, shaking his hand. "My name's Jessica."

"So," James said, "you must be pretty smart. Most kids opt for Geometry their freshman year."

"Well, I'm not a genius or anything. I'm just pretty good at math."

"Yeah, me too, I guess," he said, trying to seem cool.

He was feeling jolts of lightning in his veins as he walked side by side with this beautiful girl, Jessica. If only James knew that his life would become a series of beautiful lightning strikes, always followed by the sudden, unexpected rumbling of thunder.

Ch. III: THUNDER

James and Jessica had walked to class, spending the time talking about the 3 classes they had together. Every minute, James found it harder and harder to believe that this girl was real. As they arrived at the door, they saw the class was nearly full. Looking around at the desks, no two were available next to each other. So, James and Jessica went and sat down separately, much to James's dismay. Jessica seemed displeased as well, but James couldn't see her face as he was walking away from her.

"Freshman," said the man at the front of the room. As he turned around, James got a good look at his old, sagging face. He had grey hair combed back, and a thin mustache and goatee that matched in color. He was tall, with no visible muscle on his bones. Though his whole body was covered with black leather shoes, black socks, brown slacks, and a blue plaid button-down shirt peeking out by the collar from under a red sweater, James could somehow still picture the man's skin hanging off his body, landing on the ground near his feet. "Welcome to Algebra 1. My name is Mr. Franklinson. Don't call me Bill. Now, I'll take it easy on you guys, since it's the first day, but don't think it won't be getting difficult. Let me just pass out these Course Overview sheets so you can begin to see what my course will be like and what I'll be expecting of you." Franklinson started to make his rounds, passing out the sheets.

"Wait, what?" James asked.

"What?" Franklinson replied, just as confused as James

"Why not?" said James, from the back of the room.

"Why not what?"

"Why can't we call you Bill."

"Because I prefer Mr. Franklinson."

"Why didn't you just not tell us your first name to begin with?" he questioned. The class all looked back at him, including Jessica, all curious as to where he was going with all this.

"Student, I don't very much enjoy backtalk."

"No, I'm not trying to-"

"What did I just say? No backtalk! This is my classroom. While I'm teaching, I will not accept backtalk, sarcasm, and any other foolishness. Is that understood, James."

"Yes," James said reluctantly.

"Is that understood by everyone?" Franklinson spoke. The room uttered back a unanimous *Yeah, Sure, Whatever.*

James slumped back down in his desk, as he began to feel his stomach rumbling. He figured he had to use the bathroom. Although, having just gotten off to a bad start with Mr. Franklinson, he thought against asking about leaving the room.

"Alright, students," Franklinson began, as students got handed the class handbook. "Like any teacher, I have some basic rules that need to be followed. One is that you MAY NOT leave the classroom until I have completed roll call. Unless it is the utmost of emergencies. And I'm talking life and death, not 'really really really feel bad' or 'really really really have to go to the bathroom.' When you walk in, and you sit down, you will patiently wait for me to say your last name, and following that you may reply with "Here." From then on, you may politely ask to leave, and I may grant you passage from my classroom if your reasoning be deemed worthy. For, you see, all the lessons I have to teach in this class are guaranteed to be essential to your future, at this school, in life itself. So, whether it's right at the beginning, in the middle, or right at the end, and you ask to leave, my answer will be based on the severity of your request. My next basic rule-"

"Uhhhhh... I actually think I have to go now. To the bathroom" James said.

"Student, you have reached a new world record for fastest time getting on my last nerve. Less than three minutes. Now, -"

"My name's James by the way. And, I, like, seriously need to go."

36

"Firstly, of all the people in this room, I care the least about knowing your name in this moment. Secondly, I already knew your name, because, though this isn't your business, I have a list of all my students' names on my desk for roll call. Thirdly, in case you didn't hear me just now, there will BE no leaving until I finish roll call. Now, if you get up from that seat before the bell rings, I will personally walk you down to the principal's office and personally call your parents. Now, SIT DOWN!"

James slumped back down once again.
"I don't think I'm asking for much here," Franklinson sighed. Meanwhile, James was noticing the rumble he was feeling was rising, into his chest. He was feeling pressure from the inside against his whole body. It was starting to hurt.

Jessica turned to James from the row above. "Are you alright?" She questioned.

"Maybe," he said, wincing. James felt something bubbling up inside of him, like an intense heat, a fire rising out of his pores. It felt so real. It was as if every cell of his body was full of heat.

"Denn?" .... "Here" .... *"Fidell?"* .... "Here" ....
"Garcia?" ...

"Here," Jessica replied, looking back at James.
"James, are -"

"JUST - I'm fine," he said. The pain was all the way to his toes and fingertips. It was like he was back in the hospital, but a hundred times worse. It was enough to make someone else scream. This was the most painful thing he had ever felt.

Just then, as James was descending into agony, Jessica turned around again and said, "James, I'm- …….…… James, your skin is green."

"What?" James said. He looked as his hands and arms. They were emitting a dim, green light. It was just like the hospital. If James didn't know something was seriously wrong, he did now. "Oh my god," he said to himself, "I need to go."

Mr. Franklinson looked up at James, oblivious to his distress. "*Jenkins*?" he called.

"HERE!" James shouted.

"Okay. NOW, if you still-"

"I'm SORRY!" James shouted, jumping up from his seat and shuffling through the desks in front of him, "I HAVE TO GO!" He bolted through the door and out of the room, slamming it as he continued down the hall.

"Well then," Franklinson said, the rest of the class shocked and unmoving in their seats, "I guess it was an emergency."

James sprinted down the hall, frantically screaming, causing a ruckus enough to attract the attention of every room he passed. As he sprinted down the hall, flailing his arms, doors opened as teachers and students watched him. He ran down the stairs so quickly he would've tripped over himself if he didn't have a green hand on the railing.

James decided to run all the way home, as it was the only place he thought he could retreat to. As eyes watched him from every window in the math department, and soon all the other buildings, he left the school's campus. James turned his 10-minute walk to school into a 2-minute sprint, running as if the pain was chasing him.

He arrived at his house and practically kicked the door open. "HELLO!" he called out. "MOM! DAD!" It seemed that nobody was home. He thought he was going to cry. "I NEED HELP" He whimpered. He ran up to his room, and slammed the door. He took off his shirt, and looked at his chest. His entire torso and arms were green, and looking further, something inside was glowing. It was his bones, radiating the intense energy he had consumed when he fell into that green liquid. He was screaming at his fullest volume. The feeling was like a needle piercing every fiber of his being.

He balled up his fists, still shouting at the top of his lungs, and suddenly, an intense bubble of light was forming from them. James felt a very slight relief. He tried to squeeze his fists harder, putting every ounce of his energy into it, and a beam of light exploded from his fist, erupting with a semi-loud zapping noise and traversing the room. It landed on a small rug under his desk, and burned a hole right through it. James was stunned as he looked at his hands, still blindingly bright. He looked at the floor, then looked back at his hands, then he looked straight forward, and then he fainted.

V

James awoke. He looked around the room at all the things in their places, trying to figure out if it was a dream he had just had. His eyes soon found the smoke lifting from his rug. His reality set back in.

The beam had burned through the rug, and had almost reached the wooden floor, now singed. He lifted his wooden desk off the ground with one hand and moved the rug out from under it with the other. Along with the light beam, he also found weird how easy it was for him to lift the desk completely off the ground, what with all the books and binders in the cabinets and drawers. And what with it being a fairly large desk and all.

After a couple minutes, James finally pieced it together. It was the meteor that was making his hands – do that weird thing with light. Also, he realized that the beam of light could burn through things. For a second, he thought it was kind of cool; this newfound ability was almost like a superpower. But then, he thought about if it was a bad thing or a good thing to have superpowers. They were no other superheroes in the world. James would become an outcast; he would be branded as a freak and sent to a laboratory to be experimented on. He had to keep this power a secret. His mind racing a mile a minute, James figured that if he couldn't get rid of his powers now, he could at least harness them.

James sat on his bed and just thought. He did this for 10 minutes. He wondered how he created that beam of light, and even more, how he could do it again. It clearly happened when he was stressed, angry, and focusing really hard. The problem was that he never got stressed; not even by the surplus of homework he was given every night by his teachers in past years. James needed to figure out a way to use the ability whenever he needed to. He would have to work at it. Practice makes perfect, right?

V

James went outside, through the back door of house and onto his backyard. Hopefully the bushes and the tall-ish fence would keep the neighbors from seeing anything. He pointed his hands at the sky, thinking really hard. It wasn't working. This was going to take more practice than he thought.

James looked at his hands, imagining them lighting up. He balled up his hands into fists, practically stabbing his palm with his fingernails. Then, like a spark, one of his hands light up, and then the other did as well. His hands felt weightless. Then, his feet felt the same. That feeling shifted to his entire body. He felt like he could jump and not hit the ground again.

He would've tried, but then reality caught up to him. He remembered school, Brian, Jessica, what they would think of him. What about his parents – HIS PARENTS! James hadn't thought that the school would call them and tell them that he left without even telling his teacher.

James ran back inside through the back door. He went to the window of his living room, and saw that they were already there. His mom and his dad were coming out of the car. James did the first thing he could think of: he bolted up the stairs and went into his room. He closed the door. He heard his parents coming up the stairs. The pressure of the confrontation was killing him. He just opened the door and said, "Mom! Dad! I was... I was waiting for you." They had puzzled looks on their faces.

"Honey," said his mom, "The school called us."

"What about?" James tried to stay calm in the situation.

"Well, son," said his dad, "They said you ran out of the school, and it looked like you were sick. Are you alright?"

"I'm fine," James said. "At least, now I am." His parents were puzzled again, waiting for an appropriate explanation. "I was feeling really bad. My skin looked green. It was probably all part of a hallucination. I ran home so I could – uh – throw up."

"Doesn't your school have bathrooms?" said his mom. His dad nodded.

"Yeah, but they're really gross." James had never lied this much before.

"Okay." said his mom. "We understand your situation. We will not punish you for 'skipping school.'"

"Oh, thanks mom." James was relieved. "So, should I go back to school today?"

"No, son" said his dad. "You nearly just got out of the hospital. We both know how hard this may be for you, and we don't want you straining yourself anymore. For a while. Stay home for the day and rest. You'll go back tomorrow. And make sure you email all your teachers about homework."

"Okay," said James. "Although, it's the first day, I don't think they'd assign that much - .... I think I'll take a nap now." James could've believe he got off easy. He started backing up to his bedside.

"Alright honey," said his mom, "get some rest."

"Okay." James began to pretend the fall asleep on his bed. His parents left, and closed the door. James immediately got up, and went back to thinking about this power of his. He jumped out of bed and looked at his hands. He balled up his fists again – this time, slowly – and light once again illuminated from his hands. He opened his hands, got up, closed the blinds, and went back to lying on his bed, looking up at his bedroom ceiling, still in the greatest shock of his life.

Ch. IV: THE SUIT

James had never intended to miss the entire 1st week of school. But, green skin was the perfect symptom for such a length of absence, because it looks a lot worse than it actually was. Well, it was actually pretty bad, but James still got over it. All day, that week, when his parents went to work, James was at home, working on his powers. He would set up old cardboard boxes as targets for the beams of light he was shooting out of his hands. He wasn't yet able to hit them, though, as much as he tried.

As James was working with the beams of light, he kept feeling the weightlessness from that first day of school. He would go to his room and recreated the feeling. His hands and feet glowed bright with light, and he looked down and saw his feet off the ground. Feeling himself about to faint again, whether from the exertion of energy or the shock of floating off the ground, he would stop and lie down.

By the Friday of that week, James was able to fly up to his ceiling and stay up there for several minutes.

V

His world had been changing so fast. What he thought was fiction was becoming his reality. The previous night, while looking at comics, an idea sparked in him: a super suit. He had been thinking about being a superhero before, all through his childhood as a dream, and now as an actuality. If he were to do that, he'd need a suit. And, rather than spend all day wishing he could have one, he decided, right then and there with the comic in his hands, he should try and make one. He wanted inspiration for a cool superhero-suit, hence him reading the comics. James didn't see anything too different from the others. Pretty much all the heroes on the cover were wearing brightly colored, skin-tight suits, with designs and symbols that relate to their powers. James thought for a minute. He realized what he needed to begin. So, he told his mom he still needed some fall clothes, so that he could break away and stop by a retail outlet that he had heard about. He brought a small backpack, so, he could inconspicuously get the fabric and leave with his mom without her noticing.

On the Friday of that week, James was at the mall with his mom - which looked way more embarrassing than you think - in department store buying more fall clothes. While his mom was looking for jeans and long-sleeve shirts, James was setting his plan into motion.

While his mom slowly drifted off, he made his way to a wandering employee, who wasn't busy at all, and asked him a question. "Excuse me, sir. Where can you find spandex, in a variety of colors?"

"Spandex? Are you kidding me?" The store attendant chuckled derisively. James wasn't laughing, instead giving the man back a blank stare. The man cleared his throat. "On the bottom floor, there's a store called *Mr. Stretch: Spandex and Such*. It has a variety of colors and styles."

"Thank you, sir," James said. "And please don't tell my mom where I went, if she asks you."

"I don't care," he said. "So, why do you need spa-"

"It's a personal thing," said James. "I just need – spandex."

"Well, okay then."

James slinked out of the store and took the elevator down, just before his mom could turn around. He had told his mom he had brought his own money, so he could get a snack while she was shopping, so if she ever questioned where he had been at this time, he had an alibi. But still, if she found out he was spending his money on spandex? Questions really would be raised.

James stopped at the 1st floor and walked around the mall. He stopped in front of a store with a bright, superman-like *"S"* at the top of the entrance. He entered the store and began to look around. It was half the size of a regular mall store. There were many different shelves that held different shades of basic colors.

The store appeared empty, except for the cashier. James moved around the islands of spandex rolls and went to the shelf labeled *Yellow* and looked at the different shades. He had a bright outfit pictured in his mind. He looked at the top, and he saw a shade of yellow called "Sunshine Yellow." James thought this went perfectly with his powers. He reached up, and snatched down a roll. Then he saw "Darkness Black," across the room on the bottom of the *Black* shelf. James just thought that it went well with the yellow. He walked over, bent down, and snatched that roll up as well. James went to the cashier. He put the clothes on the counter and took out his wallet.

The cashier scanned the items. "That'll be $10.00." she said.

"Thank you," said James. He handed her two $5 bills. "Oh, and - uh - this may sound weird, but, theoretically, how do you make spandex into, possibly, –... never mind."

James left the small spandex shop, tucking the spandex rolls in his backpack. He found his mom and they left the mall.

V

After trying on all his winter clothes, James checked to see that both his parents were in the living room, and he took the spandex rolls out of his bag, unrolled them, and looked at them. He didn't know how he was going to turn the huge sheets of spandex into some kind of super suit. In most of the comics and movies and TV

47

shows, you never really saw the heroes make their costumes for the first time. They usually just skip to the action. James didn't know where to start, so, reluctantly, he asked his mom for help.

His mom was really into sewing things. At least, she used to be. James went downstairs and saw his parents watching TV on the couch.

"Mom," said James. "Can you teach me how to sew?"

"James," asked his father. "Why do you need to learn how to sew."

"It's for a school project," James quickly said. "I need to know how to turn fabric into, say, a glove or a shirt, or pants, ... or a mask."

"I'd be happy to teach you," said his mom. "Let me get my needles and pins."
James realized he had made a mistake. He should've just looked it up online.

V

After being taught by his mom how to sew, for 2 hours, James began to sew together his suit. It was Saturday, so he still had a lot of time before he would have to go to bed. He closed his door, then locked his door, and then but a chair on the doorknob of the door. He didn't want his parents barging in while he was making a superhero suit.

He used a new pair of pants and a new shirt from the mall as stencils for his suit. He cut out two pieces of paper shaped like each of the two. He made them a little smaller than the actual clothes, because he knew that spandex stretched really well. He sewed the two shirt pieces together, and then the two pants pieces together. He turned them inside out to conceal the thread line, and it actually looked pretty good. To connect the two pieces, he made a "belt" out of the Darkness Black material. He sewed the shirt and pants together, and then sewed the belt around it

Then, he made gloves, the same way he made the shirts and pants, with the black spandex. He knew he would also need footwear, so he spent the next 20 minutes cutting the black spandex out perfectly the fit his feet. He then grabbed his old pair of shoes, took out the soles, and put them in the bottom of the boots to give his feet support and comfort. He sewed the gloves and boots to his suit. The final touch was a black collar, extending from roughly the midpoint of his neck to around his shoulders and down to his upper chest. It was a masterpiece. Now, how was he going to put it on?

James stripped down to his underwear. He tried to get his feet through the hole for the head, put his ankles were stuck. James thought of something else. He pulled the thread out of the shirt, pants, and belt to separate them. He put the shirt and pants on, slipping his hands and feet though the sleeves and pants and into the gloves and boots. Both the shirt and pants were too long, so the yellow fabric around his waist bunched up. Then, he tied the belt around to hide the break in the suit. It all fit perfectly, just like he imagined. He could lose a few pounds but nothing to be-

KNOCK. KNOCK. KNOCK. "James?" he heard his mother ask from behind the door. "What are you doing in there?"

"Just working on a project, mom." James tried to hide, but there was really no place he could.

"Can I come in?"

"NO, MOM!" he yelled.

James's mom tried the doorknob. "James, why is the door locked?"

"I'm in my – uh – I'm naked."

"OH!" his mom yelped. "Okay. I'll come back later."

"Son, why are you working on your project naked?" Somehow, his father heard that entire conversation from the living room downstairs.

"It helps me think?" James was just spitting out nonsense now. He wasn't even trying to be convincing.

"Okay. Well, put on some clothes before you forget."

"I will, Dad. Thanks."

Now *that* was a close call. Well, not that close, because the door was locked. But, he almost had to explain exactly why it was locked. James almost got caught with a full-body spandex suit on. He wondered what questions they would've asked him if they had seen him. That made James remember what all – okay – *most* good superheroes need to keep their identity secret. A MASK! James went back over to the black spandex. He cut out a long strip and then cut out holes for his eyes. He held the two ends of it around his head, pinched it and removed it, and sewed the ends of the strips to each other. He put the strip around his head again. He looked at himself in the glass of his bedroom window. He looked like an actual superhero. Barely.

"I look like an actual superhero," he said to himself. There was still one thing missing from his costume, the most crucial part: some sort of symbol. An emblem which represented his powers and what he stands for. "Maye like a light bulb or something?" he thought to himself. "I'll think of something later."

James kept looking at himself. He flexed his muscles, which had just begun to appear suddenly in the last couple weeks, and made a motion like shooting something with his hand. He got a little cocky, and accidentally let off a beam of light on one of his bedroom walls, resulting in a smoking circle of black dust on the wall and causing dust to come out. The entire house shook slightly at the impact, and it all smelled like something burning now.

"JAMES!" his mom screamed. "What happened?"

"Uhhh……. I dropped my backpack. I'm fine now."

James took off the suit, and folded it into a nice pile. He put it inside the bag that he brought the spandex home in, tied the bag up, and stuck it in his closet. James was beat. It had been a long week, full of coming to terms with his new abilities, and starting to master them. Still only in underwear, and still having not taken a shower, James turned off his bedroom light and got into bed, under his blanket. Turning onto his side, he faced his open closet. As he drifted off the sleep, his eye rested on the suit, sitting at the center of the closet floor, as he wondered if he would ever really need to use it.

Ch. **V**: EVERYTHING'S FINE

James came into school the next Monday, and everybody was concerned about him. Students he'd never met or ever seen were consoling him, worried about him. This was the one time he was unhappy to be in such a "warm and caring learning environment," wishing that his school was full of cliques and nobody would talk to him. Because, everyone who walked past him would stop him to ask, "what happened to you?" Obviously not wanting to tell anyone about the abilities he had mysteriously acquired, all he was able to say to anybody was, "I was really, REALLY sick."

But then, during his Monday free period after lunch, he saw Brian, for the first time that day, in the locker corridor. "Dude, I heard about what happened in Algebra last week," Brian said. "What was up with that? Like, are you o-"

Looking at him intensely, James said "follow me." He grabs Brian's shoulder and rushes him into the janitor's closet. Luckily, the janitor wasn't there. Brian flipped the light switch on as James closed the door and leaned against it.

"Okay, what the heck is going on?"

"Brian, do you remember that camping trip I went on with my uncle."

"Yes."

"And remember how I was in the hospital?"

"Yes?"

"And remember how I told you I thought I was fine when I left."

"No, you never said that. But you were fine at school a week ago, so I figured you left the hospital in good shape."

"Well, Brian, I wasn't fine. That meteor gave me....... something weird. Like....... weird powers." Brian was speechless and confused. "Now just be quiet, and let me show you what I can do. And whatever you do, don't scream out. Nobody can know we're here."

"Ok," Brian said. "This is getting kinda weird."

James turned around and switched off the light. "What are you doing, dude?" Brain questioned, James shushing him. "Are you taking off your pants?"

"What?" James quietly shouted. "Dude, what the - Forget it. Just, watch." James closed his eyes and focuses like he did at home. His fists lit up. To Brian's eye, there were two little yellow orbs floating by his waist. Again, he was speechless. Meanwhile, James felt the feeling of weightlessness again. James was soon lighting up the entire closet with the energy from his hands. Neither could see it, because James's eyes were closed, but the whites of his eyes were glowing bright yellow. Brian couldn't believe what he was seeing, as he looked around at the walls of the illuminated room and looked back at James's blinding fists. Then James started to float above the ground. Brian squealed with excitement, and that was when James realized Brian not only got the gist of it, but was also about to go into a rampant frenzy. He stopped.

As he landed back on the ground. Brian started shouting "HOLY CRA-," but James lunged forward and covered his mouth. When he took it off, Brian started blabbering more quietly. "Oh my god! Oh my god! Jesus Christ, what is this? How did you do that? I don't - I don't - how-"

"It's my powers," James said. "These are just the things I can do now."

"Bro! This is, just, like- I - ……. So, you can fly."

"Kinda."

Brian eyes widened, and then, a very serious expression emerged on his face. He stared James down until James started to wince, waiting nervously for something bad to be said, for his best friend to disown him after he showed him the kind of freak is was now, for Brian to go tell some authority figure about all this and have James arrested and sent away to a lab. This negative foreshadowing coated his mind with an ominous glaze, but then, Brian said:

"THIS IS AWESOME!!! You really are a superhero! I didn't think it could really be this way, but it is! I mean, I was JOKING on Monday, but this is CRAZY!!!"

"What am I gonna do?"

"Well, if I was you I'd-....... Well, I'd....... Jesus," Brian said, pacing the floor. "I mean, this a lot to - I mean.... you *could* go tell your parents and they could call some specialists or professionals to make you normal." James had obviously pondered this thought before. Brian continued, "ORRRRR... we could have some serious fun with this."

"What?" James replied.

"I mean, we could figure out how these powers work. We could, like, try doing stuff with them. That would be so cool."

"See, this is why we're best friends."

"What?"

"Dude, I have been at home, all day, for the last week, figuring out my powers. Seriously. Like, as soon as I GOT the powers I was working then out. See, we are on the same wavelength right now." Brian smiled. "OH, and I haven't told anybody but you."

"That's cool. But, like, dude, I'm thinking even bigger than just mastering your powers. I mean, you could be an actual superhero with this. Like, saving lives, stopping armed robberies, getting kittens down from tall trees. JUST LIKE in the movies. Like, the whole town's gonna know who you are. Speaking of which, you need a super-suit."

"I did that too."

"Really?" Brian questioned. "Lemme see."

"Alright, well, I didn't bring it with me to school."

"Why not?"

"Well, I mean, it was just for fun. I don't think I'm ever actually going to wear it."

"James, you never know when a bad guy's gonna show up at our school and you've got a suit up and take him down.

"Uh-huh" James muttered with a smirk.

"I'M SERIOUS," Brian said. "Okay, maybe not a "bad guy," per say. BUT, think about this: more realistically, what if a school shooter came onto our campus?"

"You know, it's just called a 'shooter.' The reason school shooters are called that is because they're doing it to a school, not cause that's just what they're called." James was avoiding the recognition that Brian made a good point.

"You know what I mean," Brian said.

"No, you're right," James conceded. He thought for a moment, and said, "I....... We'll see. Maybe I'll bring it tomorrow." Brain nodded in agreement. Both then turned toward the hallway.

Brian and James opened the closet door, looking out at the hallway. It was now desolate, empty of any students. Everyone must've moved to another section of the school, as they seemed to be the only people there. They slithered out of the closet and walked over to his locker. As James was putting in the combination, Jessica, coming down the hallway, starting walking up to them. Brian turned and saw her, and for James's sake he silently and awkwardly slinked away, as James slowly opened his locker.

57

"Hey, Brian, what are you -" he said as he turned around.

"Hey, James," Jessica said.

"OH!" James jumped backward onto the lockers, slamming his door shut. "What's up?"

"I was just, checking in on you," she said. "You ran out of school pretty quick, last week. And you looked really bad....... and I haven't seen you all week, and I....... and... I... I just wanted to make sure you were alright."

"Oh, I was -" He looked at Brian, who had taken new position diagonally across the hall. "Just sick." Brian looked back with a worried gaze.

"Okay," Jessica said jokingly. "I would've guessed that." She laughed. James laughed nervously

"Yeah, I'm cool," he said. "By the way, how much did I miss last week?"

"Not that much," she said. "I mean, English was to read, History was to read, besides that I don't know, since we don't have the same teachers."

"Right," James said.

"We could go over them if you like. Oh! And Algebra, because I know you missed a lot in that class. Like, in the library someday after school, or during school if you, maybe, have another free period. We could meet up?"

"Sure." James lifted his wrist to look at it, but quickly set it back down when he remembered he didn't have a watch. "OH! You know, this is my only free period today, and it's almost up. I can't do it today. Really sorry about that."

"Oh, too bad," she said. "I guess we could do it tomorrow."

"No frees tomorrow, too."

"That's a shame," she said. She moved some of her hair behind one of her ears with her hand.

"Well, I mean, we could meet after school?" he said.

"Okay," she said. "Sure, tomorrow after school."

"Cool," he said nervously. "It's a date." Then Jessica laughed nervously. "I mean, not a date. It's like a - it's a - calendar - like a - like a date in a calendar - like, not a date like that. Like a -"

"I know what you mean," she said.

"Cool."

"Okay, so," Jessica said, "Why don't I put my number in your phone? So, if you have questions before then you can call me."

"Uhhhh... Okay." He handed his phone to her, and she started putting in her number. James and Brian locked eyes and silently celebrated. "Here," she said, giving his phone back. "So, do you want my number also?" he asked.

"What?" she asked.

"So, you can call me?"

"Well, I wouldn't have any questions about the homework, now would I?" she said, smiling.

James laughed. "Right, but…"

"Just call me later. I'll answer, and then I'll have your number," she said. "I actually have a meeting with a teacher, so, I gotta go."

59

"Okay," James said. "Well, you go ahead and do that. I'm gonna hang around here for bit."

"Okay," she said. "Do whatever you want. It's your free."

As she turned, James blurted out, "So, you'll DEFINITELY answer?"

"Yes, definitely," she said with an exhale. "Talk to you later."

Jessica walked away. As she did, Brian slinked back into frame. "Dude," he said.

"Dude," James said back. "I can't believe this is happening."

"Yeah. Like when have either of us ever dated a hot girl, right?" He sighed.

"Well, it's not a date, per say," James replied.

"Well, maybe you should ask her out for real. I mean, I doubt she'll say no. Like, c'mon, look at how she was on you like that?"

"Uhhhh... I don't know, Brian. I'll think about it," he said. "Hey, can I just ask: why aren't you more....... I don't know, amazed by my powers?"

"I don't know. It's whatever, honestly," Brian said.

"Uhhhhh... Cool." James and Brian started walking to the library.

"So, you're cool, right. You're not gonna die or anything. You've got these powers under control?"

"Yeah, I'm fine, dude," James said. "Everything's fine." James really did believe this statement, but truthfully, things around him and everybody he knew were just beginning to all turn sour. He'd just have to wait and see for himself.

"So, what do you have going on afterschool?" Brian asked. "Do you wanna hang out?"

"I'm free right after school," James replied.

"Well, I've got Cross Country, so….. How about after practice, we meet at *PepperRonnies*?"

"Why *PepperRonnies*? Nothing against that place, but can he just hang out at my house?"

"Cause I'll be hungry. Alright, see you there, dude."

"Yeah, see you later." Brian walked away, and James, standing next to his locker, retreated into the whirlwind of thoughts going on in his head.

For the rest of that school day, James tried to forget about the whole "Superhero" thing and go back to leading, or at least wanting to lead, the life of a normal person, but he just couldn't. He fantasized about being a hero. He reminisced about the last week, staying home every day, where instead of completing the assignments he got from his teachers, he was working on his powers, trying to perfect them as if they were maneuvers in a sports game or songs to be played on an instrument. Though they weren't really improving, at least he knew what he could do, for the most part. And whenever his parents left, and he was alone at home, he would go to the backyard and practice flying. James was becoming stronger every day, and starting to believe that he could go head-to-head with any of the villains from movies and comics that he'd seen and read. On the last Sunday night, when his parents were out getting dinner, just before he went to bed, he went out to the backyard, working on flying one last time. At that point, he was able to go up by his bedroom window on the second floor. In just a week, he had excelled from getting about a foot off the ground, to being able to touch the roof and come back to the ground in seconds. Thank god his neighbors don't look out their window often.

As school let out, and James started walking home, he felt a way he hadn't felt before. He felt like he was strong. Indestructible, even. He felt like he could save the world. Not only that, but that he *needed* to save the world. He felt... Powerful. In his mind, the only thing that could counter his incredible abilities was... A villain?

Ch. VI: THE ROBBERY

After sports, James met Brian at the halfway point between school and their houses. and they headed downtown. Passing all the lit storefronts of restaurants, clothing stores, and one bank, they arrived at their favorite pizza spot: *PepperRonnies*. It was a nice, little spot, run by Ronnie Alesci. To say the least, they had amazing pizza.

They stepped in and got in line for food. James liked deep dish, and Brian liked regular, so they got their respective plate of slices. They sat at one of the few empty tables.

Chewing a mouthful of Mozzarella, James looked around at all the patrons currently eating. His eyes landed on a table. "WOAH!" he shouted to James. "Dude, look over there."

"What?" Brian looked over. "WOAH!"

Two girls sat at a table in the corner of the room. One was very beautiful, and the other was Ronnie's daughter, Alexis, who was in the grade below James and Brian, at their school.

"Go talk to her, man," James said after he swallowed his pizza.

"I don't know....... I don't know," Brian said. "Ahhhh... Alright." Brian got up and walked over to the table. After Brian chatted with them for a minute, James saw Brian motion for him to come over. James got up and moved to them.

"James, this is Corrie," Brian said. Corrie, the pretty one, waved.

"Hi," James said to her.

"Oh, and this is Alexis," Brian said quickly.

"Hey," Alexis said to James. She turned to him with a wide smile on her face.

"Hi," James said again. "I don't believe we've met. So, you're Ronnie's daughter, right? I used to go to your school."

"Yeah," she said laughing. "Does he talk about me a lot? I don't come here often."

"No, not often," James replied. "But he has said some riveting stuff."

"Oh GOD!" She said, covering his eyes.

"I'm only joking," he said, laughing. "Kinda..."

Brian told James to sit down, so he did. While Brian was talking his mouth off to these girls, trying to impress the pretty one, James turned around and noticed a man with sunglasses was walking in. At first glance, he seemed to be just some guy getting an early dinner. But James looked closer, and this guy looked like he had something on his mind. And his sunglasses couldn't hide it.

"Dude," James said, trying to get Brian's attention. Brian rolled his eyes and looked at where James was pointing. He saw who James was seeing. "What's he about to do?"

"From his looks," Brian said sarcastically, "Nothing good. Look out! He's gotta coupon for two slices and a drink!" Brian said laughing, trying to seem funny in front of these girls. The girls didn't even grin.

"No. I think he's really bad," James said. He was looking at this man walk up and put his hands on the counter.

Brian grabbed James by the shoulder and pulled him in close, speaking right into his ear. "Look," Brian said, "just because you have powers doesn't mean you have to use them."

Suddenly, the man was showing the end of his gun to Ronnie at the register. Ronnie's smile turned to a frown as he looked down at the cash register.

"Oh my god, look at the gun, Brian!" James quietly shouted.

"Bro, chill. Can you just be calm? What are you even talking about?"

James turned back and the man with the gun was sprinting out of the place with money from the register in his hand.

"Oh, CRAP!" James shouted as he jumped out of his chair, knocking Corrie's drink onto her skirt.

"So sorry!" Brian said. "He's a little bit hyper," As Brian started pulling napkins out of the table's dispenser by the thousands, the girls got up and left. He angrily jumped up from his chair out the door after James.

"SOMEONE STOP THAT MAN!" Ronnie shouted as the store erupted in Chaos. "He's got my money!" Alexis shoved her way to the counter to console her father.

"JAMES!" Brian shouted, as he turned corner down the side of the restaurant.

V

James followed the man for several blocks, easily keeping up and soon gaining on him, until he man turned into an alley. As James peered in, he saw the man huddled next to a staircase to a building's back door, counting the money. James thought about how he was going to get that money back. And in the end, he had no plan. But, he did have powers. So, James just decided to leap out and confront the man.

"Hey!" James shouted at the man. The man stopped moving and slowly turned around. "That money belongs to Ronnie," he continued.

"What's it to you, kid?" the man grunted.

"It's nothing to me," James said. "But it is to Ronnie. So, how about you just give me that money," James said this confidently, "and maybe I'll let you off with a warning."

The man pulled out the gun again, and James shrunk back, still deathly afraid to use his powers on another person.

"How about you SHUT UP!" the man shouted, "And I'll let YOU OFF with a warning."

James was scared, but he was also engulfed with the flame of hatred this man brought out of him. James stuck his arms out and focused on the man. His hands lit up, illuminating the once darkened alley. The man, now scared of James, prepared to shoot. James released the pressure in his hand, and a beam shot out, which narrowly missed the man's head, hitting his arm. The man fell on the ground, dropping the gun and the money. He gripped his arm in pain, grimacing, but there wasn't any blood coming off his hands. *Perfect*, James thought, *I didn't kill him*. James ran over, picked up the gun and threw it away to the other end of the alley. He grabbed and money and turned around to walk back.

Just then, a man appeared at the end of the alley James faced.

He was tall, and wearing a trench coat. The man spoke thus:

"Hello, young man. I've been looking for you. It hasn't been long, but... still....... I've missed your presence."

James was awestruck. *Who was this guy?* he thought. "Hi. Who are you?" he said back.

"You need not know, my friend." The man inched closer to James. Now more visible in the remaining light from James hands, James saw that the name was dark-

skinned, wore sunglasses, and the trench coat was white -
like a scary doctor's lab coat.

"I notice that you have some amazing newfound
talent. Talent that I could never have foreshadowed the
existence of. Talent that is very valuable to me. How much
do you want for your powers?" This man was bargaining.
Not for money, but for abilities.

James had so many questions. He began to say,
"Uh, I don't know what-"

"What you should say," the man continued, "is, 'I
want my life.'" The man tightened his fist, which had a
weird glove on it. "For you see, your life is already in my
hands. Now, I'm not a nice guy. And you will soon find
that statement to be incredibly true if you don't comply."

"WHO ARE YOU?" James shouted.

"If what you call a "strange aircraft" gave you those
powers, I'm sure I could use similar technology to get them
back out. Wouldn't you like that, young man?"

"Aircraft?" James questioned. His desire to even
engage the man was decreasing but his curiosity was
increasing at the same steady rate. "What do you know
about it?" James was getting nervous. He moved his right
arm behind his back, beginning to light his hand up and
preparing to defend himself.

"I know a lot about a lot of things, young man," the
man said. "One thing I know for certain is that walking
around with powers like that....... well, from here on, I,
personally, would keep them to myself."

James aimed his right arm at the man and sent the
beam of light at the man. The man simply put up a hand,

and within a second, the light came back towards James, hitting him square in the chest. James fell back in pain. He didn't know how that possibly could have happened. What had this man done?"

"Listen here, boy, I don't have to tell you anything. But, I'll be nice and spill a couple of the beans. Now, let's just say... I've got things to do. And, you've got the powers I need to do those things. You - and I am deeply sorry to let you know this - you were never meant to have these powers. It was all a miscalculation. Some things simply didn't land where they were supposed to." The man was getting closer to James, his sunglasses reflecting the light from James's hands. "So, let's just-"

"JAMES?" They heard Brian say in the distance. Suddenly, the man halted his advances and regressed back to the other end of the alley.

"We'll meet again, young man," the doctor said. "I'm sure of it."

"JAMES!" Brian shouted as his head peeked into the alley.

"Stay wary, James," the man said. And just like that, the man was gone.

"Jesus, man, you knocked him out," Brian said. James turned and saw that the robber was still on the ground, practically crying.

"I guess" James said. He flexed his fingers, flashing some light in his palm.

"Woah," Brian said. "You're a superhero now. I'm not even exaggerating, like, you are a serious, actual, no-joke hero now."

"I'm not," James denied. "I'm just... helping out."

"Dude, this is - We need to get this guy back to - come on, help me move him."

James and Brian picked up the guy, each holding an end of his body. They carried him all the way back to *PepperRonnies*.

V

When they arrived, a couple cops were already waiting. James and Brian walked to the front of the store and handed the robber over to the police. The robbers' shirt had singe marks where James's hands were. The cops didn't really notice as they handcuffed him and took him into their car.

Ronnie exited the restaurant and approached them, as a crowd formed around. "Nice job, boys," he said boisterously. The crowd cheered *YAY!!!*. "Where'd you find him?"

Brian looked at James. James thought about what he said, after standing up to an armed robber and defeating him with his powers, maybe him being a superhero wasn't so far-fetched a claim. "He tripped and fell," James said. "Got hurt pretty bad. I just went up, Brian grabbed his gun and threw it away." Corrie, who had come outside with the crowd while still holding napkins to her skirt, perked up when she heard this. Brian did as well. Oh, also, I grabbed the money."

"Speaking of which, do you just happen to have that on you by any chance," Ronnie said as he leaned in, one eyebrow so high up on his forehead that it could've filled in his receding hairline if it wanted to."

"OH! Yeah," James said, pulling out the large wad of 20s and 10s from his pocket and handing it quickly to Ronnie. Ronnie looked at it for a second.

"Alright," Ronnie said to him. Then he turned to the crowd. "ALRIGHT!" he shouted again. The crowd cheered *YAY!!!*

"You guys are gettin' free pizzas!" Ronnie shouted. The crowd cheered *YAY!!!*

Then Ronnie said, "Just for these two."

The crowd groaned *OHH*.

Ronnie led the boys back into the store and the crowd dispersed, some going back to their seats and others just leaving.

James and Brian sat back down at their table. People in the restaurant came over to briefly thank them. Corrie, dress dry but still sticky, came back with Alexis and began talking to Brian again, showing a lot more enthusiasm than before. Brian accepted all the attention, even though he really didn't do anything to help. James was humble enough to let him bask in the glory.

"Thanks," Alexis said quietly to James. "Means a lot to me. ....AND MY DAD! Sorry, I meant to say my dad. But, also, it means a lot to me too." She laughed. "Sorry."

"No problem, anytime," James said. "Well, not anytime, I mean, I have school 5 days a week." Alexis giggles again.

James sat down to his free pizza, but couldn't take a bite. He thought about the man in the alley. *Who was he? Why did he want his powers? How did he know who he was? How long before the man would find him again? How did he plan to get the powers from him?* The questions plagued him in that moment. But not before long, his adrenaline lowered, and his attention turned towards less pressing issues: Jessica. The next day, he would be "reviewing what he missed last week" with her. Or so he thought?

Ch. VII: THE RENDEZVOUS

It was the next day. Between the end of school and James's "study session" with Jessica, Brian had skipped sports, telling his coach he was sick, and was helping James's train with his powers in the gym they had on campus, which was now empty. First off, he was going to figure out how to control his light-shooting without having an aneurysm.

"Just, do it!" Brian said.

"You try and shoot light out of your hand on command," James insisted.

"C'mon. I've seen you do it."

"No, you actually haven't yet."

"Whatever. All you have to do is focus on your hand, right?"

"I can't focus on my hands when bad guys are right in front of me."

Brian walked over, placing a hand of James's shoulder. "You just need to believe in yourself," he said, trying to keep a straight face and failing. At that moment, things started to click for James. Cause that's when James just put out his hand, aimed it at Brian's foot, and shot.

Brian fell over, in pain, but still laughing. "See - ow - There you - ow - Go. Jeez, that actual hurt a little. Can we take a break?"

Next on the agenda, flying. James had been getting close to it, but in those moments his focus was on staying in the air so much he couldn't possibly think of moving around.

"So, how did you do it before?" Brian asked.

"I don't know," James replied. "I just did it. I guess when I really focused, and then I started lifting off the ground.

"Okay, well, I won't try and tell you what to do this time - cause I don't want to have to buy new shoes - so, I'll just let you focus."

Brian went and sat on the bleachers. James was alone in the middle of the gym. He closed his eyes, and started to center his focus. As he did, he began to lift off the ground as he had before. Brian was amazed, as he had been before. James was up so high he was able to touch the ceiling of the gym. James looked down. Now that he knew, deep down, that he could fly as high he wanted to, he wasn't afraid to see if he could control it more. James just leaned forward, and his body started to become horizontal. As he leaned further forward, like he was falling on the ground, he zoomed faster toward a wall of the gym. James aimed his body far to the side, so as not to crash into the wall, and now he was flying around in a jagged circle, high

74

above the floor. Brian's eyes followed James, as he bounced around the walls of the gym like the marble in a pinball machine.

Suddenly, something in James's backpack started vibrating. Brian reached in and pulled out his phone. "James!" he shouted. "Phone!" Brian threw it to him. James stopped circling and zoomed to the right to catch it. Realizing that his hands were currently lit, he ended up having to stall his power in one hand to catch the phone. He caught the phone as he started falling to the ground. He landed on his feet, unharmed by the fall.

It was his father calling. He hit answer.

"Hello?" James said.

"Are you okay?" Brian whispered. "You just fell, like, 20 feet." James shushed him and put the phone back to his ear.

"Hey, your mother wants to know when will you be coming home from you date?" his father said.

"Again, it's not a date, Dad," James said. "And I don't know."

"Can I get any sort of estimate?" his father asked.

"I don't know," James said. He looked at Brian, who shrugged in confusion. "Like, 10:00?"

"Oh, staying out late, are we?"

"Talking like Yoda, are we?" he said, rolling his eyes.

"Alright. Call me or your mother later."

"Yeah, alright, see ya," James said, hanging up. "Jesus," he said to Brian.

"Was that Jessica?" Brian asked.

James's face scrunched up in shock that Brian could ever assume that. "NO!" he. said. "It was my dad."

"Oh, right, right, Brian said.

After a moment of silence, James had a realization. "OH CRAP, I didn't call Jessica. Oh no, I gotta-"

"No no no wait!" Brian said, holding out his hand to stop James from scrambling for his phone. "This is good. This shows her that you aren't obsessing. If you are going to call her, you shouldn't seem like you meant to call her yesterday. Don't sound outright apologetic because you didn't call her as soon as you possibly could."

"You think?" James said.

"Yes," Brian said. "So, you can call her, just don't be apologetic."

"Okay," James said, bringing up his phone again.

"But, if she starts sounding like she wishes you actually were apologetic, then do what you were originally going to do.

"Uhhhh…" James was confused now. "Okay, I'll just - I - I'll - I'll just call her now." James went into his contacts and found *Jessica*. He tapped her name and then her number. He looked up at Brian who was giving him the thumbs up. The line rang once. Then twice.

"Hey, has any of this ever worked for you?" James asked. The ling rang a third time. And then, silence.

"Hello?" James said.

"Hello, James?" said the other line, in a barely audible voice." **"It's me."**

"Hello, is that Jessica?"

"Yes, it's me, Jessica."

"Hey. What's up?"

"**Not much, just waiting for you to text me.**"

"Wait, really?"

"**I'm kidding,**" she said.

"Oh," James sulked back down.

"**Kinda,**" she said quickly after.

"Alright," James said, grinning from ear to ear. He looked up at Brian, who was mouthing to him to chill out and act cool. James forced his smile away, as if Jessica could see it from her house, and went back into his conversation.

"Okay so what are we doing?"

"**Studying,**" Jessica said.

"Yeah, but where?"

"**I don't care. OH! What about *PepperRonnies*?**"

"Uhhhh... I've actually been taking a break from that place."

"**Well, then I'm out of ideas,**" she said.

"Yeah, me too."

Brian leaned in. "Wait, 'me too' what?"

James took the phone away from his ear and put a hand over the screen. "We don't know where to study?" James said to Brian.

"Uhhh…" Brian began to think. James put the phone back.

"**Well, how about your house?**" Jessica asked. "**If that's fine with you.**"

"One second," James said. He moved the phone from his ear. "Uh, Brian," James said slowly. "She said my house."

"She said your house?" Brian said, smiling.

"She said my house!"

"She said your house!" Brian shouted.

"She said my house!"

"Say yes! SAY YES!"

"I'm gonna SAY YES!!! YEEEEAAAHHH!!!"

James quickly put the phone back to his ear. "Yeah, cool, whatever. I mean, if that's convenient for you."

"**Great**," Jessica said. "**What's your address?**"

James gave Jessica his address, so she could write it down.

"**Great. So, is 7:00 cool?**"

"Cool as a cucumber," James replied.

"Jesus Christ," Brian groaned, placing his head in his palm.

Jessica laughed. "**Okay, I'll see you later.**"

"Yeah, see you later," James said. He hung up.

"Alright, I think you did good," Brian said.

"Hey, man, I gotta get home now and clean up," James said. Grabbing his backpack. "See you tomorrow."

"Yeah, good luck man."

James began running to the door. He turned around, still running. "THANKS FOR HELPING ME WITH MY POWERS!" he shouted to Brian, before turning back around to continue running home, feeling a weightless kind of happiness, like he was still flying in the gym.

V

James arrived at his home, sliding his backpack off and plopping it next to the couch. He found his parents in the kitchen.

"Hey guys," he said to them.

"Hi, how was sch-

"So, Jessica's coming here now to study. Is that cool?"

"Well…" his mother began to say.

"It's perfectly fine," his father said.

"Okay," James said.

"Where will you be?" his father asked.

"In the living room?"

"Okay, as long as you're not in your bedroom or anything."

"Honey!" his mother said to his father.

"I'm just saying honey," he said, moving over to James to wrap his arm around James's shoulder, "our boy's growing up, we've gotta start expecting these things to happen."

"It's not romantic, though," James said, feeling like he had to point this out again.

"Well, whatever it is," his father said, winking at him, "it's alright with us."

"Well, okay, then," his mother said. She saw flaws in his father's logic, but refrained from mentioning them. "We can't wait to meet her," his mother said.

"Yeah, can't wait," his father said, giving him a pat on the back.

James spent the next couple of hours cleaning the first floor of his house. He only stopped when he heard a doorbell ring at the door. James jumped up to get it.

It was Jessica.

He opened the door. She was wearing a nice, medium length purple skirt, with a black-and-white letterman jacket over a black spaghetti strap shirt. She looked amazing.

"Oh hi," James's father said as he strolled in from the kitchen and walked up to the doorway. "And you must be-"

"Wow," James said. Jessica blushed.

"Nice to meet you Wow," said his father, jokingly. "We're his parents." He turned to James and mouthed *WOW*. James laughed a little. "Nah, I'm just messing with you. It's nice to meet you, Jessica."

Then his mom walked in. "OH, HI JESSICA! I'm James's mom. You're Jessica, right?" James placed his head in his palm.

"We'll just be - in the other room if you need anything," his father said.

"We will?" his mother questioned.

"Yes, honey," his father said through his teeth. He grabbed her hand and pulled her into the office as she blabbered out some muffled remarks about girlfriends and kissing.

"Yeah, those are my parents." James said, clenching his teeth. "Love'm to death."

"Okay, so…" Jessica diverted, "Let's do this… study thing."

"Yeah, I've got my books right here," he said, pointing to the couch. "Shall we?"

"We shall." Jessica and James sat down on the couch. "So, what do you want to start with?"

"Algebra?"

V

"Alright, what next?" Jessica said, frantically searching for another binder.

"Listen, Jessica," James began.

"Yeah?" Jessica said, smiling at him. James became a nervous wreck whenever Jessica looked at him like that, with her perfect smile.

"Uh - Uh - Well, I was - Uh - Look, I - Is this? - Can I ask you something?"

"Yeah, what?" she asked again.

"Why did you want to help me study, exactly?"

"Cause we're-" she stopped. "Cause we're - well, you've been absent for some time. I just wanted to be a good - I just wanted to help."

"Really?" James said. He began to say, slowly and carefully, "I thought - I thought this was more - more like a - uh - more like a-"

BRRRIIINNNGGG!!! BRRRIIINNNGGG!!! James's home phone rang loudly. He got up and stretched an arm out to the coffee table in front of them, to pick it up.

"Sorry, I - Sorry - I gotta take this?" He said, thankful that he didn't have to finish that terrible sentence he had started. He picked it up. "Hello?"

It was Brian.

"Yo! Get down here. Some guy is robbing a bank."

"Down where? And what guy? WHAT BANK!!!"

"Some guy in a long white jacket thing. I'm at *PepperRonnies* and this guy is robbing the bank across the street."

From Brian's vague description, James thought it very well might be the guy from the Alley. But, then again, a lot of people where long white coats. Nonetheless, his help was needed. "I'm on my way." He ended the call, and looked at Jessica, who quickly matched his look of distress.

"What's going on?" she asked.

"I just - I just need to go. Sorry, I wish I could stay." James got up and bolted upstairs to his room. He ripped open his closet, and grabbed the bag containing his suit up from the floor. He opened the bag, and just stared at it. This was a pivotal moment in James's life. He stuffed the suit in his backpack and ran back downstairs. As he ran through the living room, Jessica stopped him.

"Wait, why do you need your backpack?"

"I'll be back in a few. Just tell my parents I went out." He sprinted through the door, into the kitchen and past his parents, and then out the backdoor.

Once outside his house and away from any wisdom he took the suit out of his backpack. He was going to use it for the first time. Under cover of darkness amid bushes in his backyard, he changed into his suit. It took all of 2 minutes. Lastly, he put on the mask, both concealing his identity and giving him a sense of security from the real world. Then, he turned right, toward *PepperRonnies* on Middle Avenue. He started flying up and then leaned forward, just like he did in the gym. He was rapidly flying to *PepperRonnies*.

V

James landed on top of a 12-story building, the bank residing in the first floor of which. He crouched at the edge of the building. As he looked over the edge, he saw lights were on and coming from the door of the bank. He saw the shadow of a man from there. James was also able to see Brian, one of the people looking out the window of *PepperRonnies*.

James thought about what his plan would be. He was gonna jump down, land in front of the bank and look threatening. Then, he'd enter the building and confront the man trying to rob it. Without giving him a second to defend himself, he'd shoot at him with his light beam and the man would fall to the floor in pain. He'd drop the money and the police would come in, arrest the man, and thank him for his help. He would become a true hero.

James put this plan into action.

Just then, the cops showed up to arrest the man. That made things a little bit difficult for James now. Now they might arrest him as well. James just went on with the plan. He jumped down.

As he fell, he gained the attention of the cops below him on the ground. He started flying as he was falling on the ground in front of the cop cars, allowing him to land softly. He landed facing the bank, then he turned around to see the cops. They looked at him in confusion and fear. The people in all the stores that were hiding suddenly came out to see this spectacle. Brian and the rest of *PepperRonnies* Customers became nestled in a pack behind the cops. Brian looked out at the street and saw James. He was shocked. He outright said, "Oh. My. God."

"FREEZE!" one of the cops shouted. They all pulled out their guns and aimed them at James. James froze.

"Okay, guys, let's just calm down," James began. "I'm gonna go in there and-"

"FREEEEZE!" the cop said even louder than before.

"I'm gonna go in there and stop him," James raised his voice, trying to assert himself.

"Kid, get out of the street," the cop said. "We don't want you getting hurt."

"I'm NOT just some kid," said James. "I'm here to help.

"Are you some kind of superhero?" the cop said sarcastically.

"I'm just helping out," he said.

"Wow, he's really tryna make that a thing," Brian said.

After a few seconds, that cop turned around and said, "Weapons down." All other officers put down their guns. "Alright," he continued. "I mean, you just jumped off that building and floated down here like a big, yellow, human balloon, so… I mean, if you think you can go in there and stop him, go for it. We're not gonna do any better."

James nodded at the cop and smiled, then turned around and started to enter the bank. Once inside, he saw the same man from the alley, with his white trench coat and shaded glasses. He had 3 bank tellers held captive. The man turned.

"Oh, James." said the man. And with a wave of the hand, a swarm of tiny balls of metal erupted from a band on his wrist and into the air, and were sent flying against the entrance. The door was then closed by the metal balls and the man was keeping it that way. James was locked in. "So good to see you after our little - talk." He looked James up and down. "I like the get-up. Did you get those threads from Mr. Stretch by any chance?"

"Why are you robbing a bank?" James asked.

"Because, I'm a *baaaad* man. Also, I was hoping you'd show up to meet me here. I've probably been driving you crazy since you met me."

James hated to admit, but this guy really had been driving him a bit crazy. "Well, I'm here," he said. "I wanna know why you want my powers."

"That's not important," the man said.

"Actually, it kinda is."

The man threw another wave of metal at James that stuck him to a wall. James was restrained. He shot a beam at the metal on him and it quickly fell off, scurrying back to their master in clumps. James fell onto his hands and knees, but quickly got back up. The man was impressed.

"Well that's neat isn't it?" The man said. "You know, I'd like you to do something for me………….. Shoot me." The man stood there with his hands down.

James was weirded out, but wasn't going to pass up this chance to take this guy down. He shot straight at the man with his light. The man shouted in pain and staggered to the ground, holding his chest.

"Ah," the man said through its teeth. "Not strong enough to kill but enough to keep me at bay." The man got up and shook off the pain. "That'll REALLY come in handy."

"What's your problem?" James said. "You think you'll just capture me and drain me of my powers?"

"Why not?" The man said. "That's all I need of you. Actually… You know what? That sounds like an apt strategy. Why didn't I think of that?"

"So, you're gonna kill me, huh?"

"Well, I'm not trying to kill you, really. I just want those… those pesky powers."

"How would you even drain me of my powers? How do you know enough about me to even think you could do that?"

"Oh please, James. You don't remember me in the slightest? Not an inkling of a clue?"

James said nothing.

"After your accident, remember that guy that was checking up on you.

James was confused.

"Do I… remind you of anybody?" After more silence, the man lowered his glasses down the bridge of his nose, revealing his eyes. Suddenly, James saw it all. The white trench coat, the short black hair, the thick glasses, looking like a scientist. It was Dr. Dean, from the hospital. Or, at least, the man who called himself Dr. Dean.

"You were my doctor," James said, staring blankly at him. "What do you know!?!"

"Please," he said. "Call me DR. DARK! You like that? I thought of it myself."

"What do you know about me!?!"

"More than I know you wish I did," Dark said. He raised his hand and the metal that James had previously shot at rose up again and were flying towards James in a big mob, but James was able to dodge it. After averting the attack, James sent one right back. It hit Dark square in his face. He stumbled down a little, turned around and took off the glasses, which were now broken and singed. Looking away from James he said, "Fine. I'll leave. I don't want money anyway. I just wanted your attention. MORE OF IT, at least." He straightened up, "If you don't let me have what I want, I will not be happy."

"Oh, you poor thing. You won't be happy? Aren't you a little old for temper tantrums?" James questioned.

"YOU MOCK ME????" Dark shouted. "I MOCK YOU!!!!!!!!" He sent a flurry of metal at James's face, causing him to cower away. Dr. Dark then pushed James aside, and sprinted ahead to the doors. He slammed them back open, and shot all his metal at the cops. All of them were covered in the little robot pieces. The crowds backed away. James now saw the scope of this weapon, spread out across an entire police force.

Dr. Dark created a tall wall of even more metal from his wrist, between him and the cops. After 20 seconds of the cops frantically trying to escape their metal traps, the wall then fell, as did all the metal covering the cops, and everyone on the street saw the Dr. Dark had made his escape. James then looked over at the cops. He could've tried to stop him, but he was still scared of his abilities, still unsure of his potential. The cops looked at him.

"Well," James said, slowly backing away, "I guess that's my cue." James looked up and started flying, up and away from the crime scene.

Nobody there knew what to say. What do you say after seeing someone land in front of you from the top of a building without a scratch, shoot light out of his hands, and face off against some evil doctor with metal coming out of his wrist watch. They were all shocked.

V

James landed back home. He came around to where we left his backpack. James took off the suit, his gloves and boots, crammed it in his bag, and he put his clothes back on.

James slowly opened the door. He looked around. "Mom? Dad? Jess?" Nobody answered. He sat down at the couch.

"James?" his father said. James looked over his shoulder. "Over here, dad," he said. James looked back forward. He caught his reflection in the TV, which was off, and saw he was still wearing his mask. He quickly took it off as his father came in, and stuffed it under his leg.

"So, how'd it go?" he asked.

James was confused. Did he know about the bank? "Uh, wait, what?"

"How was your "study" thing?" he said, smiling.

"It was fine," James said, oddly relieved. "We studied. We talked a little. Uh - where is she? Did she leave?"

"Oh yeah. You were gone for a while. She said she had a curfew, and she really wanted to stay and wait, but her parents would kill her if she didn't get back home. So, yeah. She left."

"AW CRAP!" James exclaimed. He held his head in his hands, looking down at his feet in dismay.

"Yeah. She said you 'went out.' Where exactly did you go? And why didn't you get our permission first?"

"JAMES!!" his mother shouted. "WHERE WERE YOU!!! You had us worried sick!"

"I just went down to *PepperRonnies*. Brian said some guy was breaking into a bank. I wanted to see what all the fuss was about. It's not a big deal."

"Jessica said you were worried," said his mother. "Like it was urgent."

"Oh no! I just - uh - didn't want to miss it."

"Ok. Well," his dad said, looking at his mom, "I guess it's fine. Just let us know before you go out next time. It is past 9:00. If you really need to be somewhere, just let us know.

"HONEY!" his mom said to his dad.

"Hun, he's 15. We can let him have his freedom. In a few years, he'll be out the house completely. So, let's start weaning him off our constant care now.

"Thanks, Dad," James said, still in shock from his encounter with the man called Dr. Dark. "I'm gonna go upstairs and get back to studying."

James ran up to his room. He took the suit out of his backpack and laid it out on his floor. Then he pulled out his phone and tried to call Jessica. She didn't answer. James tried twice more. No answer. Finally, he turned off his phone. He looked back down at the suit. It was a little dirty, but nothing he couldn't wash out. He folded it back up and put it in his backpack.

As James got ready for bed, his phone rang. It was Brian. He picked up.

"Hey, man, I am-"

"YO YOYOYOYOYOYO! I CAN'T BELIEVE YOU JUST DID THAT!"

"Man, I gotta go to bed. I am BEAT!"

"Hey, real quick. Sorry I started off with that, but I actually really need to tell you something that just happened. And, you're not gonna like-"

"Listen, man, I am seriously tired. Whatever it is, can you tell me tomorrow?"

Brian remained silent on the other line for a few seconds.

"You still there?" James said.

Brian came back. **"Yeah, sorry. Uh... Okay, man. I'll see you tomorrow."**

"Yeah," James said.

90

"**Yeah, definitely**," Brian said, hanging up. James threw his phone onto his nightstand, not a real care in the world about what he said. He could only think about Jessica.

As he climbed under the covers, he wondered how the next day would go, seeing Jessica after he ran out, and seeing Brian after the Bank Incident. He knew it wouldn't be a very good or easy day, but if he knew what he was really in store for, he wouldn't have gone to school at all.

Ch. VIII: THE CLOUD CAVERN

James came to school the next day looking for two people: Brian and Jessica.

As he walked onto campus, he saw Brian walking into the main building. James ran after Brian. James reached Brian, but before he could get his attention, a swarm of people came through, playing a video of James in his suit at the bank on their phones. He heard mumbles of people saying, "Did you hear about the light guy?", "Who is he?", "How did he do that?", "Where'd he get those powers?" Now that he thought about it, James heard the whole school talking about it.

Brian turned around to see James. "James," said Brian. He looked around before leaning in and quietly shouting, "THAT WAS THE GREATEST THING I'VE EVER SEEN!!!!!! YOU JUMPED DOWN IN FRONT OF THE COPS AND FOUGHT THAT EVIL GUY! THAT WAS INSANE! HOLY-"

"Well," James cut him off, holding his shoulder and

bringing him down as if that would lower his volume, "It wasn't that great. I let him get away."

"Yeah, but you put up a fight," Brian said. "That's better than any of those cops could've done."

"I guess when you put it that way-"

"Dude, everyone is talking about you. They just don't know it. Someone filmed it and uploaded it to YouTube. It's almost hit a million views. I think it's at, like, 950-thousand something-"

Jessica was walking across the hall. "Jessica!" James suddenly shouted. She heard her name and looked in that direction. When she saw who called it, she rolled her eyes and kept walking.

As James started to get ready to sprint, Brian shot out a hand to grab his shoulder. James stopped, and turned around. "Brian, I gotta go."

"James, I really need to tell you that thing. Like, right now. I'm serious."

James broke free of Brian's grasp and turned back to the hall. "JESS!" James said, running after her. When he caught up, she turned around to see him. "Jess, I'm sorry. Something came up and it was more than I thought it was!"

Jessica looked at him, staring with dead eyes. "Only my friends call me Jess."

"Oh, c'mon, I'm sorry."

"Just -" she stopped. Her face turned from an angered look to disappointment. "You know, I actually....... kinda liked you. But, now I see you're really not my kind of guy."

"NAH! NAH! Wait, please listen. What do I have to do to -"

"What? To do what? I waited there, on that couch, for two and a half hours. Your parents kept coming in, asking if I needed a ride home, and I would just say I was waiting patiently for YOU! I got home at 10:30. My parents were so mad at me."

"Hey, I -" James didn't know what to say. "I'm sorry."

"Just get a tutor next time" Jessica turned around and left him there in the hall.

Brian slowly walked up behind in. "James, I need you to listen to me right now."

"Brian, I gotta- "

"James, there's other girls in the grade, okay?"

"Yeah, but I wanted her." James said.

Brian spoke quickly. "You're gonna be fine. But RIGHT NOW, I NEED to TELL you this!"

"Brian, what?" James said.

Brian was silent for a second, just looking a James, wondering exactly what to say. "Okay, look. It's... I'm sorry, man, but... Look, it's about Jessica."

James's mental focus made a 180 turn from Jessica to what Brian just said: Jessica.

"WAIT WHAT?" he questioned loudly.

Just then, a sea of people formed down the hall, of people trying to get to their lockers before first period. In the middle of that sea, looking out above all the students, stood a very, very tall man, that looked all too familiar.

Both James and Brian looked over to the man at the same time.

Brian said, "Dude, is that -?"

"IT'S THE GUY!" James shouted.

The students all looked at the once inconspicuous man. Dr. Dark shouted back, "Aw, you gave me away!" Suddenly, several other men in lab coats and glasses came out from a classroom and ran right into the crowd. Each of the henchmen grabbed a student and gripped them tightly by their clothes. One of them was Jessica.

As faculty and other students now crowded, Dr. Dark spoke to the whole school:

"Students, teachers, the person I am looking for, the one, lone, young man, is in this school." James held his head down while still intently looking up at him. "If he doesn't show himself now and surrender to my forces, I will take these students. So, it's quite simple, really: five students or one student. I'm sure there are some math teachers here. And the rest of you can all take out your calculators if you want, but I'm pretty sure, just guessing, that if this one student comes forward, you will have a whopping 5 MORE STUDENTS! That's quite the offer. Anyway, still waiting for that one student. Make your move, if you're out there."

James looked at Brian, scared. Brian looked at James, scared. Jessica looked right at James, scared. None of them were moving. Nobody was moving.

"So be it." Dr. Dark started to turn.

"WAIT!!!" Dr. Dark heard someone shout. He turned back and smiled with one eyebrow up. The crowd all turned to the student, including James, Brian, and Jessica. "I....... am Light-boy." All were silent, as James's eyes shifted around in confusion.

"Very well," Dark said, approaching the student. He held out his hand for the boy to shake it. When the boy went for it, Dr. Dark grabbed him and sicked his wave of metal on the boy. It came out of the very wrist holding on to the boy's arm. The boy was covered in the metal. It picked him up, and slammed him against the lockers, dropping him down beside them unconscious.

Everybody winced in pain at the sight. But then, all were relieved, and began murmuring somewhat positively.

"....... That wasn't the kid, in case anyone was wondering," Dark said.

The crowd groaned *OHH*.

"Suit yourselves. Since no one wants to come forth, I'll just be taking these 5 kids with me. And... I know you're here, boy." Dark turned his head towards James, but with the shades on no one saw the piercing stare being given to James. "I'll be waiting for you." Dark turned toward one of the walls beside him and sent a wave of metal at it, which burned a large hole from it. Dark walked through the newly-constructed exit, and the henchmen followed, hostages in hand.

The crowd of people slowly followed. Outside, Dark and his henchmen had a large aircraft waiting for them right outside. This aircraft was eerily similar to the one which crash-landed by James's campsite all those weeks ago. First the henchmen got on with their captives, and then Dr. Dark got on. Before they flew away, Dark

looked dead at James and said, "Your move, *students*."
Then, the aircraft flew straight up, way up past the clouds,
in the span of a few seconds. It was like hyper speed.

The students started to make their way back inside
and all began taking out their phones to call their parents
and tell them what was happening. The teachers put the
school in lockdown mode, and were making calls to the
parents of the children who were taken.

Brian and James were in a different world: the
world of people who knew that a certain student really was
in the crowd, and that student could save the day.

"James," Brian said, "Can you do this?"

"C'mon, really?" James whined. "Why me?"

"Cause you can fly."

"You know what I mean? Why do I have to be the
one to save them. I mean, if it was one person, maybe. But
this is crazy."

"James, look at me." Brian held James's shoulders
and looked him dead in the eyes. "You have powers. You
have an offense to any defense this doctor guy can put up. I
saw what you did at the bank. You can FLY! You can
REALLY fly! Are you kidding me? That already puts you
above any one of us mortals down here. But your greatest
power.... is heart." James laughed. "I'm serious, James.
You've got a bigger, warmer, better heart than Dr. Dark.
And that, my friend, is why you're going to save those
students."

James stared blankly at that hole in the wall,
debating with himself for a few seconds before saying to
Brian, "Okay."

"Alright," Brian said.

"WAIT! What was that thing about Jessica you were trying to tell me?"

"Uhhh…" Brian was stuck.

"Okay, you know what, man? Just, tell me when I get back down. Seriously, tell me."

"You're sure you're coming back?" Brian said.

James thought for a second. "I've got to."

James ran out of the crowded part of the hall, turning down the corner. He found an empty bathroom and ducked into it. He changed into his suit. Then, he put on that mask, and once he did that, he was filled with the spirit of a hero again, ready to save the day.

James threw his backpack up on a high window sill and came out of the bathroom, sprinting back to where the crowd was, now all back inside the halls. They looked at him in awe, many instantly pulling out their phones to film him. When he reached the exit, he looked back. The only person he focused on was Brian, giving him the thumbs up. James smiled, then looked back forward. He placed one foot up over the wall, and then stepped the rest of his body through the hole. Once outside, he started flying up into the sky to catch that doctor.

V

James was flying so high, it was like he was up in an airplane. As James was looking down at the clouds, he realized this was the highest he'd ever flown. James then looked forward. He saw this.

It was a large building, nestled above a sea of fog that formed into an artificial cloud. It was built of grey bricks, with several windows and a grand entrance at the bottom of the building's front. It looked like it could fit into any city's skyline and look normal, but the fact that it was in the air, on top of a fake cloud, is what made it freaky.

As if he flipped a switch, James started zooming towards the lair, his success or defeat becoming more imminent every second.

As James approached, a legion of tiny ships came hurtling towards him. James shouted "Woah!" and quickly descended in flight to avoid them. They flew past him. Though he avoided their immediate attacks, they turned around and headed back. James shot at one of them. The beam pierced through the metal and sent it twirling down to the ground. James was relieved. He saw the others still coming. James sent a beam at each of the ships, taking each one down.

James figured there'd be reinforcements, so he hightailed it to the entrance of the building.

James landed and opened the door. As it opened, there were no alarms, or anything. James was able to enter the building unharmed. He looked around. He was in a large, entrance hall. The walls, floor, and ceiling were made of black bricks. There were many long staircases leading the different doors up on a ledge. James slowly inched into the room. As he started going up one of the staircases, a fleet of henchmen came out of all doorways. James geared up to fight them. He started shooting at all of them, but his beams just bounced off their chests. As they circled in, and his fear was rising and bubbling, James felt a flame building inside him. He felt himself heating up, and he felt the energy starting to burst out, from his eyes, ears, mouth, fingertips. He then stretched out his entire body and released a gigantic wave of light, blinding and scorching the soldiers around him. He fell to the ground, shaking and writhing.

Henchmen kept coming out of the doors, and it was all still too many for James to face. And by now, James was drained somewhat of his energy. James kept firing off beam after beam of intense light, but two men finally got to him, grabbing hold of his arms. They each put a heavy, metal glove on his hands and locked them into place. James kicked up and used his feet to push back the men trying to grab his feet, but they got hold and put on boots of the same material as the gloves, locking them on. James was starting the feel the weight of the gloves. It was weird how heavy they were. James began to feel woozy. As James lost consciousness, he saw Dr. Dark slowly coming down the staircase on the far left.

Ch. IX: RISE

James awoke in a cage. The metal gloves and boots were still on him. James looked around. He was in what looked like a large control room, with a large screen and many lit buttons on a desk-like interface on the far-left side of the room. Right next to him was another cage. In that cage, he saw the hostages from his school. They all looked scared, but now that he was awake, they were slightly relieved. *It was him*, they thought, *the guy from the video*.

"Aw, you're all awake." Dr. Dark said. "How did you sleep?"

"Look, you've got me here. So, tell me what you're going to do!"

"Give it time, my child." Dr. Dark said, menacingly and melodically. "What you should be worrying about is where you mask is." James frantically cowered away, trying to get his hands up to feel for his mask but finding them completely stuck to the ground. "Relax, I'm joking" Dark began again. "I didn't touch your mask, it's still on your precious little face. See, that would've ruined all the fun, now wouldn't it? Frankly, I don't care who knows who you really are. But... I see that you do. So, I'll let you have that, at least." James was relieved, but still in fear.

"LET US OUT, YOU FREAKIN' NUT!" one of the hostages shouted. They were being restrained by Dr. Dark's metal pieces on their wrists and ankles.

Dr. Dark went over to the shouter. "Do you want to say that again." He pointed his hand at the student and shot metal right at the student's face. It covered his mouth. The student whimpered, unable to speak.

"Okay, OKAY! Jesus!" James shouted. "Look, I followed your orders. I'm here, now let the students out."

"Oh no!" said Dr. Dark. "But you didn't come here to surrender, did you?" James looked down. "You came here to get rid of ME! BUT NOW YOU CAN'T BECAUSE I'VE FINALLY GOT YOU!" Dr. Dark put his face right up to the cage. "And you... You have my powers. ... I... want them."

"They're not your powers!" James said.

"BUT THEY WILL BE!" Dr. Dark inquired. "I've got you all figured out, Light-boy."

"Why didn't you just do all this when I was in the hospital?"

Dr. Dark smiled at him. "In many ways, it would would've been too easy. I mean, you could barely move. But, in another way, it was more difficult, what with all your relatives in the room who I didn't want to kill, and you were still a highly volatile subject. At least here, I don't care what happens to you students over there, and you also seem to have become very accustomed to your gifts."

Dark ran over to the table with the buttons. He pressed a couple of them and some gadgets appeared from a dispenser in the wall. James looked over at the other cage and whispered, "Do. Not. Worry. I. Will. Save us." They all looked distressed, but Jessica was the only one he saw crying. He had to do something. He just had to.

Dark came back with his gadget. It looked like one syringe, connected to a large suction cup attached to a long bending metal pipe, and all that connected to another HUGE syringe. James gulped a big dramatic gulp, imagining what he was about to do with those needles.

"Listen," Dark said to James, "I've got an agenda. And sadly, that involves killing you."

"You're actually gonna kill me? I thought you said you didn't need to take my life."

"Well, ask yourself this: will taking all the blood from your veins and all the energy from your muscles kill you? If your answer is yes, then… yeah." he laughed maniacally.

As Dr. Dark walked back to his control tower with the mysterious apparatus, James leaned over to the other cage.

He whispered the Jessica, "Hey, do you happen to know anybody named Brian?"

"What?" Jessica whispered back.

"I just…," James whispered still, "I heard about something. Nevermind, let's just not die."

Jessica was confused, but before she could ask any question of her own, Dr. Dark came back around with the apparatus. He walked to James's side of the cage. He grabbed James by the arm and aimed the little syringe at his arm. James was unable to keep him from pricking him with the gloves and boots on. "Relax," he said. "I just want A SAMPLE!" Dark stuck him with the needle, and extracted some blood. "It's like a vaccine. I just need to test to see that your blood won't kill me." Dark put the needle in his arm and pressed in, breathing heavily.

"Why didn't you do THAT in the hospital, you freak?"

"JUST SHUT UP!!!!" Dark shouted.

"I still don't know why taking my blood and energy would give you my powers?"

"You don't know much about your powers, do you?" Then, Dark dropped the syringe, and picked up the suction cup and stuck it to James chest. The gloves were inhibiting him from defending himself. "If I sat you down and revealed all the nooks and crannies full of information regarding your powers and what that green liquid was made of and why it landed near you and not where it should've, we'd be here for hours. And you've probably got places to be, so I don't want to hold you up."

"What are these gloves made of?" James said, still quite woozy.

"Clearly something heavy," Dark said. "Now SHUT UP! This is the moment I've waited far too long for." Dark put the small needle connected the suction cup in James's bicep. It should've hurt more, but James had become much stronger than an average person.

As the hostages in the other cage looked on in silent shock, and demise was closing in on him, James felt something in him again. Suddenly, he wasn't woozy. He was empowered. He felt that fire in him again, brought out only by his fear. But it was too late to do anything.

The doctor stuck himself in the chest with the big needle. As he fell to the ground in pain, he pressed a button on the tube and it began to light up. The process had begun.

James immediately felt it, like the energy is his entire body fleeting from his cells. He felt his power being taken away through the tube. Meanwhile, Dr. Dark was rising above the ground, a swirl of light and fire circling him. "YES!" he shouted. "I AM POWERFUL!!!!!" As James started sliding all the way down to the ground, losing energy and consciousness, he looked over at Jessica, looking right back at him with the same fear in her eyes, if not more. This was what he needed to see.

He picked himself up off the ground, pushing himself on the heavy gloves and boots to be standing once more. He felt the power inside him becoming stronger than it ever had before. He began to surge with power. His whole body was tingling, like that day he first got his powers. His skin was practically breaking at the seams, as light was seeping out of him. Dr. Dark saw this, and rather than halt the power-transition process, he continued, thinking that he could get even more power by these means. Obviously, even he didn't know everything about these powers. James was about to break free. The gloves and boots on his hands and feet become very hot, and soon melted off in heaps of liquid metal and glass, leaving his glowing limbs to shine through. Then, James looked up at Dr. Dark, still floating. On Dr. Dark's face, there was an expression not unlike the one that was on James's face only moments ago: fear. But whereas fear strengthened James, it only weakened the doctor. Dark saw that everything he had worked for, searched for, fought for, was crumbling in his hand and falling through his spread fingers.

James shot his light all through the side of cage, creating a hole. He then stepped out into the open, and looked at Dr. Dark. Dark was trying desperately to take out the needle, but it was now too late for him. James was nearing his fullest power. He centered all his energy, from his arms and legs and chest and neck, every ounce of energy he could muster together short of that keeping his heart beating, and sent it through the tube into Dark. Dr. Dark was, at first, feeling powerful and fulfilled. But then, the power kept coming. Dark was grabbing frantically at the tube, but it wouldn't come out. Death took off his glasses, and his eyes were painfully yellow. Light was bursting from his skin, ripping it apart and showing the binding force that had been accumulated within him.

Then, there was an explosion of such brightness and magnitude, that everyone was blinded, even James. They all could be sworn that at that moment Dr. Dark had combusted, and had been completely vaporized from existence. The explosion went all through the building, busting out every window and cracking every brick. The control center at the far-left end of the room was completely destroyed. No one felt it yet, but the building was just beginning to lose power and start falling. The intense light finally faded, as James started to cool back down. What stood there was a horrific sight.

It was Dr. Dark. His lab coat was frayed and burnt in several places. He was missing hair, and had long, deep cuts and burns all over his face and hands and assuredly everywhere else. Dark had been broken down. But, he was not... dead... yet. Still, Dr. Dark tried to fight him with whatever power he had taken from James. He held up his chest with a scorched forearm, and sent a small beam of light at James. James dodged it, and shot right back at Dark. The shot was not overpowering at all, but Dark had been so ruined, it sent him sliding back, against one of the walls.

The henchmen all came in. There were about 15 of them now. They all ran towards James, shooting at him with their blasters. Now having reached a higher level of power, James was able to take out one of henchmen with one blast, shooting one right through his chest pad and hitting him in the stomach. As the one henchman fell, the other 14 stopped for a second, and then started running away. James turned his attention back to Dark.

Dark very slowly picked himself up, and stood facing James. He stepped in front of the window to be right in front of him, and began to talk again. "You think I will be your only enemy," he said as he coughed heavily. James slowly inched towards him. The hostages in the cage started to feel the building falling. Dark continued. "You're special, Light-boy. I can be sure that you will be followed all your life. Not just by people on my team, but EVERYONE! People will not stop. They'll never stop. You don't deserve those powers. YOU DON'T DESERVE THEM! YOU NEVER DID! I KNOW IT! And once more find out why, they'll all know it too. What I've given you…is priceless."

James was fed up with Dr. Dark. He shot a continual beam at Dark one more time, and Dark was pushed back so hard he was slammed right into the window behind him and he broke it. James's light soon blinded everyone again, including him. Though blinded, James made out Dr. Dark. When the light started to dim, James saw Dark leaning over the edge of the broken window. When the light completely faded, and everything came back into focus, all that remained was some ashy pieces of cloth and a couple whiffs of smoke. James was shocked. Did he just kill Dr. Dark? Or, did Dark just kill himself?

Suddenly, the building began to start falling fast. The hostages were losing footing as they rose to the top of their cage. James had to grab at the floor to stay on his feet.

"HELP US!" shouted Jessica. "THIS BUILDING'S COMING DOWN!"

James jumped over to the cage. He held onto one side of it with one hand. With the other, he burnt through the cage. He helped the students all get out of the cage. As he did this, they were lifting off the ground. This building was really coming down. James jumped over and looked out the broken window. There was no way he was gonna be able to carry all these people and safely land them on the ground. But, he had an idea.

"HEY! EVERYONE! COME IN CLOSE!" James shouted. All the hostages followed his orders and formed a tight circle around James. Jessica was so scared, she clung to James, with her arms around his torso and laying her head on his chest. James, for a brief moment, was happy. But then, you know, the building.

James sourced his full power once more. He created a ball of light around his hands, and centered all his energy on this ball. As parts of the walls were falling off and the building was essentially turning to rubble, the ball of light started growing into a bigger bubble, and he had soon formed a bubble of light large enough to go around all the hostages. James did it. Now, all he could do is hope that this would keep them safe as the building fell.

It did.

The building kept falling, and it was so fast, James had to really put in his energy to maintain the bubble. As the building soared downward through the air and clouds, the hostages all clung to James for dear life. What was left of the falling building looked like a skeleton of what it once was. The floor was completely gone, giving James and the students an unmatched view of the ground readily approaching them. The bubble was falling like a meteor.

Finally, everything was coming down into the middle of a large, empty courtyard. Thankfully, no one would be hurt in the crash; well, maybe the henchman would feel something. The light bubble was able to protect James and the students from dying, as the building broke apart around them when they hit the ground. Once they hit the ground, James was able to release the bubble. They all touched down without a scratch. James was on the floor, practically dead. It took all his power to do what he had done.

Ambulances and police cars rushed onto the scene. James awoke a minute later, sore everywhere. He leaned up and looked around. People were coming into the courtyard to see what had just happened. They were all cheering for him. He got up off the ground, going around to help up the hostages.

Apparently, every news network had cameras on the building as it fell from the sky, because within minutes of the crash, every news network was there, with a herd of news vans hurrying in satellites. Camera operators and reporters all hopped out. They all began to speak about how James defeated Dr. Dark. A female reporter who stood out spoke thus into her camera:

When we last saw the ever-elusive hero affectionately named "Light-Boy", it was in the viral video he was featured in which has now garnered 6 million views, where he was seen stopping a bank robbery being committed by the man called "Dr. Dark" in recent police reports. What you viewers just saw was this masked boy land on the ground with several civilians amidst the remains of a building that's fallen from the sky. This building is speculated to have been the lair of Dr. Dark, a criminal who's been wreaking havoc in the city unnoticed for several months. It wasn't until last night, when Dark was found breaking into that bank, that police first discovered his appearance as well as his supposed identity. It was

also last night that the world discovered this boy, who has some unique abilities, to say the least. Yesterday, everything happened so quickly, that many people were speculating that the video was a hoax. But after this broadcast gets out, we will all know that this amazing boy is real. He is currently behind us. Let us now go to "Light-boy" to ask him where Dr. Dark has gone.

The reporter of this network, along with several other reporters, turned around and began to approach him. James was taken aback at first, but then started walking towards the cameras, not knowing which one to walk towards.

But then, Jessica ran over to him. "Thank you for saving us!" she said. "Oh my god, thank you!" Thank you so much!" She grabbed his face and gave him a great, big kiss on the lips. It wasn't an "I love you" kiss. It was like how your parents kiss you. But it was still a kiss. And James's first, at that.

Jessica and James separated. And then, both blushing, they saw the cameras that were being shoved in their faces. Jessica was frozen as she realized she just kissed James live on several news networks.

"Is this live?" she asked. All the camera people unanimously nodded. She let go of James's face and sprinted away, looking for her family in the crowd.

"Light-boy," the reporter began, "Do you know where Dr. Dark is now? Is he dead or alive?"

James couldn't think. He heard the question, but could still only think about Jessica kissing him. He remembered shooting him. But he never saw that he was officially dead. He only saw him leaning out of the window before the building fell. But with all power in the building lost...but what about the henchmen he let run away...but what about… but… James's mind raced. He really didn't know. But he had to give them something to leave him alone.

He looked at the camera and just said, "I vaporized him." Then, he backed away from the cameras and lifted himself up several feet in the air. Still within earshot, he shouted down to the reporters, "I'M JUST HELPING OUT!!!" Then, he flew up into the air away from the scene.

"WHO'S UNDER THE MASK?" the reporter shouted back to him in the sky. The cameraman said *cut* as the reporter dropped her mic and walked back to their van.

Suddenly all the vans dispersed. And in their place, came the parents of the stolen students. A hundred feet in the air, James looked down as Jessica and the others found their parents and hugged them. He was satisfied, he was elated, he was a hero……. and he was tired. He headed back to his house to tell his parents he was alright and to take a well-deserved nap.

V

It had been two days since the incident, and the school was still ecstatic. After seeing classmates be taken away to a building in the sky, and then see them on the news, surviving the crash, lying in rubble next to someone they saw in the viral YouTube video, shooting light out of his hands - and on top of all that, knowing that same boy is somewhere in their school- it can be hard to focus in class. Even some teachers couldn't focus. And it didn't help matters that is was Friday. Many teachers couldn't get a single word out, since every time someone mentioned "light-boy," a loud, long conversation started and seemingly never ended until the bell rang for the next class.

Between classes, James was looking for Brian, to hear what he had to say about Jessica. But, he ran into Jessica first. He saw her walking up ahead in the hallway. He ran up next to her.

"Hi," James said.

"Hi," Jessica said back.

"Listen," James began, "I can't say anything I haven't already said, but I want you to-"

"It's fine, James," Jessica cut him off. "It's all fine. I'm over all that stuff. I mean, you made mistakes, and I made mistakes, but...I now know that life is too short to dwell on little things like that. So, if you're willing to try not to do what you do that night again, then I'm willing to forgive you for it."

"Yeah, I'll never do that again!" James said quickly.

"Alright," Jessica said, smiling, "then I forgive you."

"So, we're cool?"

"Yeah, we're cool," she said.

"Alright," James said. They continued walking down the hallway.

"So," James said. "You and that light-guy kinda had a little moment at the crash."

"Yeah," she said, blushing. "How'd you know?"

"Uhhh……. It was on the news," he quickly blurted out. "SO, you seem completely not in shock after a near-death experience."

"Yeah, well, I didn't die."

"Hence, '*near*-death'."

"And now that we know that guy is around, what's there to be scared of?"

"Putting a lot of pressure on him, aren't we?"

"James, he's amazing. He can do anything! He's - he's so hot, I can't even lie to you. I'm sorry."

James had the widest grin now. All he wanted to do was tell her everything. But, he knew he couldn't. Dr. Dark took Jessica and he didn't even know that James liked her. He couldn't imagine what would've happened if Dark knew how he really felt about her.

"So, how cool are we exactly?"

Jessica laughed. "I don't know...as cool as we were before all this?"

"So," James continued, "Do you have a thing going on with this guy? Like, a serious thing? Just curious."

"I wish!" she said. "But no, we don't." She laughed again.

"Uhhhhhhhhhh...okay. Well, I remember when - when - uhhhh……. you - you said you - you said you li- when you were mad at me, you said you li- you said you kinda liked me."

"Uh huh?" Jessica said.

"Well, I feel like now - you know, now that we're cool again, maybe you want-"

"Are... are you....... are you asking me out?" she questioned.

"Uh...yes," James said. He didn't know much about girls, but what he did know is that when a girl has to ask if you're asking her out, she's gonna say no, one way or another.

"I'm sorry, did Brian not tell you?"

"Uhhhhhhhhhhhhhhhh.............. Brian?" James said, still not ready for whatever bomb was about to be dropped. "No....... he didn't tell me anything....... why?" There were only a few hypothetical reasons why Brian would ever be involved in this specific exchange, and none seemed all that appealing.

Then she just said the words. The one group of words James never expected to hear and never wanted to hear. Never. Even after Brian's constant warnings about something he had to tell him, James never would have thought it would go this way.

"Well....... Brian and I are going out tonight."

James was frozen. "Oh," he forced out of his mouth.

"Uhhh... Yeah. It just happened a couple days ago. Like, after I was at your house, and I was heading home, he saw me, and I was – so – and-"

"It's fine," James replied, calmly, looking down at his feet. "I just thought I would ask if....... Nevermind, it's fine." Suddenly, every dream he had, every minute he spent talking to her, every minute being in a room with her, every time he looked at her face, her hair, imagining her leaning on his chest as he had his arm around her shoulder, imagining being able to kiss her on the cheek whenever he wanted, imagining being able to say he had a girlfriend, it all became empty. Wasted time. His soul caved in, and instead of popping back out after a few seconds, it just stayed there. He didn't know what to say, and didn't want to say anything.

"Sorry about that, I guess," she said.

"Don't be," James tried to reassure her. "I just thought I'd ask." James just backed away from her and turned around and walked to his next class. Once he turned a corner, he saw Brian way down the hall. James couldn't bear to see him, thinking that if he approached him he would either break down in tears or put a smoking hole in his chest. After all the help he gave him with Jessica, James never would've thought Brian also had a thing for her like that. He felt the most betrayal he had every felt in his life. Just then, Brian looked up, jolting his vision to James. He started to put up a hand to get his attention, as he quickened his walk. James quickly darted around the corner, into some random classroom, waiting for Brian to pass. Thank god that wasn't the classroom Brian had a class in. After slowing down in front of the door, and looking around, he kept on walking forward, head hanging in shame. Once Brian passed, James came back out and quickly kept walking. He was now angrier that he *didn't* confront him. In that very moment, the anger in his heart was so powerful, he had to put his hands in his pockets, so nobody would see them lighting up.

V

James came home with many different emotions in his head. For example, he was happy to be famous everywhere and have his whole school love him. Well, not him, but the boy in the mask. But then again, he was also sad, about Jessica. He really thought she liked him. And in the end, she really did. But, why couldn't she just say yes? To him, not Brian. What happened? He thought he and Jessica were cool. Weren't they? It had to be all Brian's fault. Because, she never showed interest in him before this. Maybe she was hanging out with multiple guys. But, still, it was clear none made advances because she was so attached to James, ever since school started. So, again, it had to be Brian. Why did Brian do that? Brian knew he liked her. This was all so out-of-character, for everybody. Then again, James did just start shooting light out of his hands a few weeks ago, and that wasn't ever indicative of his character.

James didn't ever want to see him again, but he knew he would have to. What if Brian called him? What would James say to him? More importantly, what would Brain say? James had no idea. No idea at all.

James went up to his room, and took off his backpack. He pulled out his suit. And just looked at it. He had a moment of calmness in his now hectic life. He looked at the center of the suit. He wondered, thinking back to that reporter, calling him "light-boy," everybody calling him "light-boy,": He wondered what his actual superhero name should be, because "light-boy" wasn't catchy at all. James immediately remembered what he said to that reporter, about what he did to Dr. Dark.

He remembered everything Dark said. About his powers, about the aircraft that crashed near him, about everything. James's questions still lingered. Like, who really was that man? Why did James, of all people, end up with these powers? Who were they really meant for? Were they for him? Why did he need them, how was that green liquid engineered to give him powers? Who created it? Why? And when Dark was gone: did he die? Or is he out there lurking still, healing his wounds and preparing another attack on the city. *Only time will tell*, he thought. *As much as I'd like to know now, I can't dwell on it. Life will keep on going, and I just need to roll with the punches.*

Dark said there would be others. There would be others who would try and take him down. Whether it be to absorb his powers or simply to end him, more would surely come. And James would be ready for them. People knew of him now. And not just in this city, but all over the country, all over the world he was known. James now had a duty. He must use his powers for the good of all, because no one else could do what he could do. As much he didn't want to remember anything Brian said, Brian did always tell him he was a real hero. Not until today did he really think it himself. If he could vaporize Dr. Dark from existence, then he could do the same to anyone in his path, any evildoer, anyone who threatened the lives of the people he cared about. He could vaporize them all.

In that moment, before he started his homework, he knew what his name should be. More importantly, he knew what he was, and he knew his purpose. He walked over to his closet, and picked up what was left of the roll of Darkness Black. He picked up and placed a pair of scissors in his other hand, and used them to cut out a large black letter.

V.

THE STORY BEHIND THE STORY

VAPORISE began in the 3rd grade. The 3rd grade was the first year my best friend, Gideon, wasn't in my class. Thus, I realized that I was going to have to find someone else to talk to and hang out with all day. That person was Alex. We were already good friends, but this year was different. We had a shared interest in making stories and drawing, so we just started working on art and stories together, any time we could. At the Gordon School, whenever it was raining or very windy and cold, we had indoor recess. That meant that we had to stay in either our classroom or the other 3rd grade classrooms. I used to hate when this happened, because who wants to stay inside for recess? But soon enough, these would become my favorite days. Because on these days, Alex and I got to work on comic books for 20 minutes straight. On one of these "indoor recess" days, we sat side by side at one of the desk islands, as we always did, and laid out all the paper and colored pencils we had grabbed. We had already made a handful of comic books at this point, so we weren't new to this. I remember how we used to make all our books back then: cover art first. We would fold up several sheets of paper, put 2-3 staples down the middle of it. And then, we decorated the cover art like nobody's business. After that, THEN we would begin making a story. VAPORISE was no exception.

The cover for VAPORISE began as a man, whose face we didn't color in, with a flat top haircut, and he was wearing a yellow jumpsuit with black gloves and boots; it was like Mr. Incredible, but just yellow instead of red. The man was off the ground, one foot higher than the other. The

121

entire VAPORISE concept and story was originated simultaneously by both of us, starting with the name. I don't remember exactly who thought of the name "VAPORISE" itself, but what I do know is two things: 1. neither of us knew how it was correctly spelled, and 2. both of us knew it was perfect. At the time, it was a dumb typo made by some 3rd graders, but looking back, it was a stroke of accidental genius. I'll explain why later. Anyway, after we wrote "VAPORISE" at the top in bold, we opened the book and started writing.

In the end, we wrote three VAPORISE "books" in total. And by "books," I mean about 15 pages that are each half-words, half-drawings. If you put all three of our comic books together, the storyline roughly makes out that of my novelization. This is the series of events based of our books:

Book 1
- James is camping with his Uncle
- Meteor falls next to their site
- James goes near it, and falls into it, waking up in the hospital
- A doctor examining him says he'll be fine
- James goes to school, meets Brian at school, both see Jessica
- James bumps into Jessica later, he helps pick up her books, their hands touch, and they blush
- James goes to class with Jessica, he starts feeling sick, and turning green, he runs outside, and then starts flying
- James flies back to his house, and falls asleep

- When he wakes up, he realizes he can shoot light out of his hands.

Book 2

- James learns how to use his powers, figuring out how to fly and how exactly to shoot the light
- His dad finds out, and both agree not to tell his mom (This may come into play in VAPORISE II, if there ever is one)
- James goes to school the next day, he sees Jessica
- Just then, Dr. DEATH (Yes, that was his name in our books), who is implicitly the same doctor who examined him earlier, bursts through the wall and snatches Jessica, taking her up to his cloud lair

Book 3

- James runs outside and flies up to the lair
- James gets inside the lair, and finds the suit of one of Dr. Death's henchmen
- He puts on the suit. And on his chest, he burns in a large V (No particular reason why he does it)
- Just then, Dr. Death's henchmen run out and capture him

- Dr. Death cages James, putting him right next to the cage Jessica is in.
- James breaks out, and he shoots Dr. Death in the chest, sending him through the window behind him, never to be seen again

- James gets Jessica out of the cage, and flies her down to safety
- James is a hero
- CLIFFHANGER: Meanwhile, Dr. Death may not actually have died

You can see where I took liberties with the original transcript in my novelization.

V

In the 7th Grade at Friends Academy, we were assigned the Independent Writing Assignment. I had never planned to make a novel version of VAPORISE, but when I found out this would be due, VAPORISE was the first source I looked to for an idea.

I didn't have a copy of the book. Even today, I think Alex has the original comics somewhere in his house, if he still lives there. So, I just went off my memory. The above bullet points are what I remembered. From there, I just started from the beginning: the campsite.

There was a page limit for the assignment. I think it was 25. But, I went nuts, and wrote 40 pages. This was only the 1st half of the story. The due date was coming up, so I stopped writing at the end of Ch. IV, when he finishes the suit. As I said in my dedications, finishing this, handing it in, and getting back that grade is the proudest moment of my life. Mr. Walach truly did tell me he would love to see it finished. So, if you've gotten this far into my book, you already know where this is going.

V

When I came to Germantown Friends School, I planned to finish my book before I graduated. During for month of January, the high school does this thing called "January Term." During this, every student abandons their regular classes in favor of a completely different curriculum, containing classes like "Meteorology" and "Nutrition" and "Abnormal Psychology." One of my minors was "Creative Writing." The class ended up being just like a study hall, where kids came to do other homework or literally just sit there on their phones. But, that didn't stop me from getting back to my novel. I wrote the majority of the second half of the book in that class, but I also used every free period and almost every lunch to keep writing. By the last week of J-Term, on a Tuesday or Wednesday, I had finished the novel. Or so I thought.

My sophomore year, once again during J-Term, I went back to the book, and I proofread the entire thing, making edits all throughout as I went. This is when I changed Dr. Death to Dr. Dark. I felt like Dr. Death wasn't original enough. Also, dark is the opposite of light, James's power. I essentially recoated it with my evolved skill level and view of the world. I was able to add certain details into the book that I may not have been able to if I hadn't completed my freshman year. Around this time, my dad started telling me about getting this book published. By the end of January AGAIN, I had finished the novel. Or so I thought.

V

My junior year (a.k.a. this year), I went back ONE LAST TIME to proofread: fix grammatical errors, fix continuity errors, overall just make it better. I was doing this very slightly and gradually during the year. As I was working to finish it, my dad told me that I NEEDED to get this published before the end of the year. Throughout the year, I had been researching self-publishing methods and different sites to go through, and how to prepare my text for self-publication. So, once I was through with the grueling first semester of my junior year, and winter break began, I cracked down, and really got to work finishing this. In the first week of January, I officially, and I mean officially, finished the book. It was perfect. Or, at least, as perfect as it could be at this point in time. Because, as my dad told me, if I kept coming back to this book every year, instead of just letting it be and putting a stamp on it, I would just keep editing it, because I can only keep thinking of new ways to say things, and new ideas for story. And you know what? He was completely right. So, that year, I did as he said. I "finished" it. Then, I wrote all my dedications, I wrote out my copyright page, my "About the Author" section, and then I typed the words: "and then I typed the words: 'and then I typed" .....

You get the point.

I put all the pieces together into one document. I ran it through the publishing site, looked at it in the preview, and then I took it back out, fixed all the formatting problems, and then put it back in. Then, I created my book cover, I wrote a synopsis for it, and then Bing. Bang. Boom. Book published.

V

Allow me to finish all this with a few words about the name of the hero, and the title of this book.

As I was writing the first half of the book back in middle school, I thought about the core values exhibited by James and other characters, and I contemplated what the moral of the story was. There wasn't exactly a "With Great Power…", but, somewhere in there, there was a moral. I didn't know quite what. All I knew was that I wrote a story that I wanted to be true, and to live in. I wanted to be James. I was James. And if James was me, then he had to have good morals.

Speaking of morals, this is where the whole "VAPOR<u>IS</u>E vs VAPORI<u>Z</u>E" thing comes into play. I realized all this my freshman year, when I was rewriting it in January.

You see, back in the 3rd grade, that's just how Alex and I thought it was spelled. I learned the correct spelling WHILE I was writing the story. The first time I typed the word, which was on page 1, it was underlined red. I right-clicked it, and to my dismay and surprise, it WAS spelled with a Z. The reason I never changed it is because 1. It's a unique way of spelling it that I didn't want to change, 2. I thought it was more pleasing to the eye with an S, and the most important, 3. VAPORISE ends with the word "RISE." I think that's so perfectly poetic and meaningful. I never planned to have it work out this way, but the fact that it did was like destiny. Because, the word "rise" is such a strong word. It means so much: To get over sadness or anger, to overcome fear, to rise to the occasion, all things that VAPORISE stands for. Throughout the book, he does these things, and the entire book leads up to him doing those things. That was when I knew what the moral of his story was. The story of VAPORISE is the story of rising. You won't find that in the book. I never said it in what I wrote back in 7th grade, I didn't say it freshman year, and I still haven't said it in the version which finished just a few pages ago. I shouldn't have to spell it out. If you read the story of VAPORISE, and you resonate with him, and if you wish that you could be that kid who gets superpowers, makes their own suit, and fights crime or some crazy supervillain, if you wish you could bump into whoever is the prettiest person in your school and have them instantly fall for you, if you wish you could overcome your fears, and be strong enough to fight back against the forces that seek to take you down, to take what you have from you or make you feel like what you have isn't good enough.......

.......if you feel those things, then you're James too. And the story of rising will soon be yours.

Thanks for reading.

ABOUT THE AUTHOR

Sekou Hamer was born in Boston, Massachusetts, but moved to East Providence, Rhode Island at the age of seven. There he spent most of his childhood and began his adolescence. Always going to the schools his father worked at, he's spent each section of his education at a different school: early childhood at Charles River School in Dover MA, elementary school at The Gordon School in East Providence RI, middle school at Friends Academy in Dartmouth MA, and high school at Germantown Friends School in Philadelphia PA. Sekou has a strong passion for the arts, including acting, writing, filmmaking, singing, playing multiple instrumentals, and performing in general. He aspires to be an actor, planning on going to college for a BFA in Acting, but also planning to keep learning and excelling in filmmaking and writing both fiction and screenplays through college, however possible. *Vaporise: The Novelization* is the first and only book Sekou has ever completed and published. He plans to continue writing, already with ideas for a *Vaporise* sequel, as well as dozens of other completely different stories.

Currently a Junior at Germantown Friends School, he now lives in Philadelphia, with his mother, father, and younger sister.

VAPORISE
WILL RETURN